SYDNEY J. BOUNDS

THE CLEOPATRA SYNDICATE

Complete and Unabridged

LINFORD
Leicester

First published in Great Britain

First Linford Edition
published 2007

British Library CIP Data

Bounds, Sydney J.
    The Cleopatra syndicate.—Large print ed.—
Linford mystery library
    1. Perfumes—Fiction
    2. Detective and mystery stories
    3. Large type books
    I. Title
    823.9′14 [F]

    ISBN 978–1–84617–637–1

Published by
F. A. Thorpe (Publishing)
Anstey, Leicestershire

Set by Words & Graphics Ltd.
Anstey, Leicestershire
Printed and bound in Great Britain by
T. J. International Ltd., Padstow, Cornwall

This book is printed on acid-free paper

THE CLEOPATRA SYNDICATE

Maurice Cole, the inventor of a mysterious new perfume, is found murdered. But his employer's only concern is to recover the stolen perfume . . . He hires Daniel Shield, head of I.C.E. — the Industrial Counter Espionage agency — who is aided by Barney Ryker and the beautiful Melody Gay. The trail leads them to Egypt, where Shield must find international criminal Suliman Kalif and recover the perfume before the Nile runs red with the blood of a Holy War.

1

Thunderbird One

Jay Orbison shot the cuff of a pink shirt — silver links monogrammed SD — to stare greedily at a thin silver watch. The hands appeared motionless. An hour since *Isis* must have berthed; he'd watched the motor yacht round the point at Fort Tourgis. What was keeping Kalif?

From the curved bay window he looked out over heath-clad cliffs, the gannets on Garden Rooks, foaming sea. The sky was grey as it so often was, Atlantic-grey.

A wall mirror reflected a dapper little man — dapper was his word, his image — in a grey mohair suit of executive cut, beard freshly barbered to a point; an outsize domed head. He stared intently at his reflection; there was no sweat on his forehead even though he felt it crawling there.

He stood between a desk and the

window; a wide desk, empty except for intercom, notebook and a silver vase holding pencils. Hidden in the desk — delicious thought — a bottle of Scotland's finest malt whisky. His throat was parched as the Western Desert, but he didn't want Kalif to smell booze on his breath. The hell with Kalif; he was the boss here. Decision. He moved his castored chair and opened a side panel, poured a tumblerful and rolled it round his mouth, swallowed.

His pulse raced, steadied again.

A quick glance in the mirror. Despite high heels built into handmade shoes, despite the whisky, he wished — not for the first time — that he were taller. Orbison didn't like to feel small. He removed tinted glasses, gratified by the sudden radiance of his psychedelic tie, and polished the lenses.

Christ, it shouldn't take an hour to get from the harbour. Kalif was purposely making him wait, making him sweat. And when he'd cast his horoscope that morning, the omens had been favourable; the stars indicated that his affairs would run smoothly. Somehow it didn't feel that way.

The intercom purred and he reached across and thumbed a button. Virgo's silky voice came: 'Mr. Kalif and — er — party.'

'Admit them. At once.'

The party arrived first, door bursting inward to reveal in silvered italic script: *DIRECTOR*. Two dark-skinned men bounced through, one each side; they weren't carrying guns in their hands but it was obvious they usually did.

Suliman Kalif followed silently, and Orbison shrivelled as he took in the size of him. A mountain of muscle, hump-backed, wearing denim battledress; a cigar ground between solid jaws, close-cropped black hair and oily skin. He towered like a bear and looked as powerful. But it was the eyes, cold and hard as stone, that finally frightened.

Orbison clutched at waning courage — he was the boss here — and made a smile. 'Welcome to Stardata House.' His voice came out reedy; clearing his throat, he forced volume into it. 'A pleasant trip,

3

I hope?' He stepped round the desk, hand outstretched.

Kalif ignored both the hand and the greeting. Statue-still, his glacier-smooth gaze chilled. 'When can I collect?' The voice, too, was stony.

Orbison swallowed. He hadn't anticipated this kind of pressure. 'Not here, certainly, and not now. You get the V.I.P treatment, it's expected. I'll show you around and explain the set-up — later we can have a private talk.' Nothing, he realised, was going to look right about this man's visit, but he had to go through the actions. He mopped his face and sweat came away.

Kalif stared into him, silent, till he all but broke, then nodded. 'Okay, but keep it short.'

Orbison took a long breath and eased his way to the door. 'This way, please.'

In the outer office, the decorative Virgo — silver wig and miniskirt — froze at her keyboard, fascinated by the giant hunchback and his escort. Eccentrics were nothing new at Stardata House, but this trio was way-out.

4

Orbison passed in a flurry, wanting to avoid involvement. Get it over quickly. He wished he could cut the tour, but that would look even odder. All V.I.Ps got the tour; and Kalif was allegedly here for a personal reading.

He led the way down a short flight of stairs and went along the passage like a hare; the building was compact, on one level, except for his private office perched like an eyrie on top. At the end were twin swing doors and a notice:

STRICTLY NO SMOKING

He paused outside, remembering his guest's cigar. 'I'm afraid our equipment's sensitive. You'll know about that so, if you don't mind . . . '

Kalif dropped his still burning cigar where he stood. Orbison crushed it with his foot, dropped the butt in a wall tray. He pushed open swing doors and the bodyguard moved smartly through. Kalif waited, then followed Orbison.

Inside, the air was dry and cool. Grey metal cabinets lined one wall. There was a low electronic hum as an operator pecked at her keyboard, mingling with the muted hum of air-conditioning.

Scorpio, the programmer, half-rose from his seat at the control console. Orbison made a hand-signal and he sat down again.

'We handle the bulk of our work here. A computer is ideal for routine forecasting — it's fast and keeps costs down. And business is on the increase, we get four or five sacks of mail every day. Of course, my own readings are still done by hand.'

Kalif looked round with a bored expression, growled: 'You think it makes any difference?'

Orbison shuddered; that was the kind of comment he could do without. Nervous, he abbreviated his spiel. 'There's not a lot to see, actually. Input here, memory storage at the back, output over there. That about covers it, I think . . . time for our private chat. If you'll come this way.'

He led the way outside, along a concrete path between the main building and a high brick wall. The air was fresh, invigorating, but the wall cut off most of

6

the wind; the sound of the sea pounding at the rocks below seemed almost distant.

'Alone if you don't mind. I can guarantee your safety here.'

Kalif studied him coolly, then motioned his escort to drop back.

They followed the path to a second, smaller building and Orbison took a key from his pocket, and unlocked a door. He opened it on warm dry air, a distinguished smell.

'My private sanctuary,' he said, and smiled. 'Like Garbo, I sometimes want to be alone. And there will be no eavesdroppers here.'

Once inside, he shot a bolt. The interior was spacious, heated and wall-lit, wired off into compartments. The main area, totally enclosed by wire mesh, was a large aviary; Orbison and Kalif stood in a service passage. More than a dozen birds sat on perches, frozen into stillness, watching them.

'They're always quiet when I bring a visitor.' Orbison was in good humour, in control of the situation now. 'Watch this.'

The birds were foreign, coloured

midnight blue and dusky green, with long sharply pointed bills.

From somewhere came a quiet mechanical *click* and a glossy glass bead dropped to the sawdust floor and lay gleaming there. A sudden whirr of wings, like a small thunderclap, and one of the birds lifted from the flow on invisible wings, carrying the bead overhead to a nesting box,

Kalif's tone revealed interest. 'Very fast. You make use of a natural instinct, of course. Clever. What are they?'

'They're something of a rarity, from Central America. The Indian name is Thunderbird, from the noise of their wingbeats.'

'Perhaps we can now get down to business? How soon can I collect?'

'Forty-eight hours.'

'I have need of some haste,' Kalif returned mildly.

Orbison firmed his voice. 'It's already laid on. I know exactly where the vial is and my contact's been prepared. All I have to do is pull the strings, fly over and collect, bring it straight back here.

Forty-eight hours is the minimum time.'

The giant hunchback looked at him, looked back at the birds. There was another mechanical click, a glass bead falling. He nodded agreement to a beat of thunder.

★　★　★

The moon was full and bright as Maurice Cole moved with long-legged strides through the backstreets of South Wimbledon. There was little traffic, and fewer pedestrians, and he made no attempt to conceal himself.

Excitement pulsed through his veins. Confidence made him bold; everything was going to work out. Above London's hazy sky, stars twinkled like guiding lights — and they were guiding him tonight.

His latest forecast had been clear enough, now was the time to act . . .

This is your moment of destiny. Do not hesitate to break routine — events are in your favour. Success can be yours, everything you've always wanted. Reach out and grasp your opportunity.

Cole was a lonely man, tall with thinning hair; but he was clever at his job. He had a better appreciation of what he'd found than ever Grevil would have. Grevil had a small mind, obsessed with sex . . . look at the way he'd treated the Thomas girl. Cole despised him; he saw the bigger issue. There was money in his discovery, big money. He wasn't getting any younger and if he didn't make the break soon he never would.

But he was making it. *Now*. This minute, striding past a row of smoke-grimed terrace houses, an antique shop, a travel agency. His step faltered briefly as a fluorescent poster caught his eye. The Bahamas . . . perhaps he could take a holiday first. He passed windows glowing eerie-blue where television displayed canned dreams.

Maurice Cole, too, had his dream; enough money to set up his own small lab away from the Grevils of this world, somewhere he could devise experiments that interested him without interruption. And now his dream was turning into solid reality.

Grevil hadn't an inkling of the offer he'd been made; his contact had emphasised the need for secrecy. Jay-O's forecast chimed perfectly with the timing of the offer; this was the determining factor that had finally persuaded him to accept. When the stars determined a certain course of action, only a fool ignored them.

He followed a weathered brick wall to the factory and only now did he look around him. There was no one about, no lights showing inside. He had his own key and let himself in by the side gate. It was shadowy, quiet.

He crossed the yard, passing the lab where he'd spent so much of his life. Grevil kept the vial in his office, not even locked away. He went directly along the passage, opened a door. Moonlight shone in through a window onto a desk. There was a smell of polish.

Cole opened a drawer in the desk, took out a small vial shaped like a swan and almost full with a violet liquid. He made sure the vial was tightly stoppered, pocketed it and walked out without

11

bothering to look up behind him.

In the street, he looked carefully round. There was still nobody to observe him. Whistling softly, he cut through back-streets, past the café where he usually lunched, a betting shop. Opposite the tube station he caught a bus that passed through Wimbledon and climbed the Hill. Here the character of the area changed for the better, the houses were bigger and sat in their own grounds. He checked his wristwatch; twenty minutes to rendez-vous.

The bus purred along Parkside, past the ponds on the common. He got off at Windmill Road and walked between twin rows of trees. The Clockhouse was in darkness and there were no cars; the gate shut at sunset. He lengthened his stride, enjoying the walk, enjoying the idea of the freedom money would buy him. Not even a pair of lovers showed.

Further on, the windmill made a pleasing silhouette against the moon and he went past it, across the deserted car park to the trees beyond.

A wind in the trees stirred shadows and

Cole paused and peered into the gloom. He felt suddenly alone, miles from anywhere. One of the shadows resolved into that of a waiting man. Cole didn't know his name and wasn't interested.

'You've brought the money?'

'Of course.' The voice sounded faintly amused. Hands opened a briefcase, displaying bundles of notes fastened with elastic bands. 'You'll find the amount correct. My principal doesn't welsh on a deal.'

Cole's pulse pounded. So easy . . . he wished he'd asked for more. He brought the vial from his pocket. 'This really works — you have to be careful how you handle it.'

'I know. I've been briefed.'

'You won't be sorry,' Maurice Cole exchanged the vial for the briefcase, started to count bundles. 'Don't try to open the vial,' he warned. The money seemed to be correct and he wondered if he was supposed to say anything. He groped for words, but the other man spoke first.

'Is that a satellite?'

13

Involuntarily, Cole's head jerked back, his face fully lit by the moon. As he looked up, something dark flashed across the face of the moon. He felt sudden pain in his face, dropped the briefcase and flung up his arms. Jagged flashes darted behind his eyes and he buckled slowly, like an empty sack. A faint groan sagged from his lips.

He was dead before he hit the ground; and he died without learning what it was that had struck him down.

2

I.C.E.

He was a dumpy little man with a bald head and his loud check suit gave him the popular image of a bookmaker. He came scurrying with short quick steps from the direction of Jermyn Street, turning into St. James's Square, darting between lunch-break office workers. He paused only briefly in his violent haste to scan door numbers. The play of sunlight on white Georgian houses and the plane trees in the square meant nothing to him.

He located number Thirteen A and headed straight for it. This was a high narrow building between more imposing façades and looked as if it had been squeezed in as an afterthought. He climbed steps to an open door and a bronze plaque lettered:

I.C.E.

With, in smaller script below:

Industrial Counter Espionage

He padded along a short passageway to a reception hall that was long and narrow, with open stairs at the rear. It had wall-to-wall carpeting, a contemporary decor including some striking water colour sketches of the Australian outback. A couple of deep armchairs faced a desk with a switchboard; there were potted plants and reference books on a shelf, a round wicker basket with a lid.

A girl sat reading at the desk. Not really reading, he decided; just flipping pages — looking for the dirty bits no doubt.

She slipped a marker into place, put down her book. Green-tinted eyes surveyed him with cool detachment. 'Yes? Can I help you?'

'My name's Grevil,' he said. 'Nicodemus Grevil.' And looked her over.

Eighteen? No, older than that . . . twenty-five perhaps. A slight figure, reddish hair cut urchin-style. Jeans and a sweater that didn't reach to her navel, tanned; easy to

16

imagine her riding pillion to one of the chopper boys. No bra, he realised, and licked plump lips.

'You can call me Nick if you like — I'm a devil with the girls.'

'What can I do for you, Mr. Grevil?'

'Well, I've called to see your boss. Shield, that's his name, isn't it?'

'Mr. Shield is the senior partner.'

'Then let him know I'm here.'

'Mr. Shield is out just now. Can I help?'

'Anyone else around?'

'No. Just me.'

'All alone are you?' Grevil sniffed delicately. 'Fleurs du Mondes . . . I like that. I could go for you.'

'Why don't you sit down and tell me why you've called?'

Grevil moved away from the visitors' chairs, towards the desk.

The girl watched him thoughtfully, bent over and opened the wicker basket. She lifted out a big snake, six or seven feet long. Sleepily, it coiled round her outstretched arm and looped about her shoulders, lifting its head to stare at Grevil.

The snake began to hiss and he stumbled backwards, hit the edge of an armchair and unexpectedly sat down. 'Is that thing dangerous?' he asked hoarsely.

'Suki? Not unless she's annoyed.'

Grevil began to think he'd made a mistake. 'Who are you exactly?'

'Melody Gay. I'm a partner in Ice.'

'Partner, is it?' He stared in fascinated horror at the rippling body and weaving head as Melody reached behind her for a reference book. She checked something, closed the book and looked at him again.

'Well, Mr. Grevil, will you confide in me now?'

Grevil nodded. 'Of course . . . d'you think you might put your snake away now?'

'I think so,' Melody said casually, suppressing a smile. Surprising how the wolves backed off when confronted by Suki — a python was a girl's best friend. She carefully coiled the snake inside the basket and closed the lid.

Grevil relaxed and his voice returned to normal. 'The fact is, I own a perfumery — a small one — and I've had a perfume stolen. It's a new blending with unique properties. I'm willing to pay twenty thousand to get it back and I can write a retainer for two thousand now. Interested?'

Melody said quickly: 'Plus expenses, of course. What's so special about this particular perfume?'

'Reasonable expenses . . . and that needn't concern you. What you're looking for is a glass vial in the shape of a swan — it's quite distinctive and you're not likely to mistake it when you see it. The perfume it contains is violet in colour. Don't open the vial when you recover it — pass it over to me intact.'

'Where was it stolen from? And when? Any ideas on who might have taken it?'

'It was stolen from my office, at the factory in South Wimbledon last night . . . don't you want to take notes on this?'

'I've a tape recorder running.'

'Oh, have you?' Grevil thought back furiously, trying to remember if he'd said anything he shouldn't have. Just when had she switched on? He hadn't noticed

— must be foot controlled. Quit worrying, he was paying the money, wasn't he?

She asked: 'Who recommended us to you?'

'Chief Inspector Emery.'

Melody arched an eyebrow at the name. Emery wouldn't be concerned with the theft of a bottle of perfume. Something smelt. She watched Grevil write a cheque, read it through and gave him a receipt.

'Why don't you just make some more of this perfume?'

'It's not as simple as that.' Grevil's eyes refused to look at her as he spoke. 'Only my head chemist knew the exact blending. He made up only this one batch, as a sample . . . and now he's dead.'

★   ★   ★

The lunchtime crowd had cleared as Daniel Shield came up the steps of No. 13A, his head filled with chess strategy. It had been a hard fight and a satisfying one; a day when he had seen clearly — as the fact that he'd lost to a Grandmaster in no way spoiled his pleasure.

He went along the passage, wondering
. . . suppose he hadn't played his knight
to KB7 on the twelfth move? He
visualized the board but couldn't see
anything better. It had given him a fork
with a double attack on the queen; yet the
move had led to his downfall. Borg was
just too good for him . . .

He glanced round the reception hall,
noting absently that Melody was out;
something must have come up. The lid
was on Suki's basket and he was amused
by his own feeling of relief; he still had to
exert conscious control over his fear when
the python was loose, despite Melody's
insistence that snakes were warm. Dry
and entirely lovable.

He climbed the stairs and unlocked the
door at the top. Beyond was a small
landing with his office directly opposite.
He went in and sat down at his desk, a
tall man with dark hair and sympathetic
brown eyes. A mature man, big but
well-proportioned, wearing a heather-
tweed suit.

He switched on the tape Melody had

left and listened to her interview with Grevil, and her comments on their latest client made after he had left.

'Grevil strikes me as the unscrupulous type — I'm not sure we should trust him very far — anyway, first stop the library.'

Shield had a mental picture of Melody in the back of a cab, turning pages, fixing each page in her eidetic memory. She would have a mass of factual data on perfumes stored away in her mind before she reached the factory.

He lit a king-size and sat thinking. A stolen perfume, a new blending, a dead chemist — and Emery. The presence of Chief Inspector Emery made it murder.

He dialled Scotland Yard and asked for Emery; he and the Chief Inspector were old friends and he got the information he was after. Emery was still out on the case, most likely at the victim's home. Shield spoke the address into the tape recorder and added a message for Barney.

He looked up again and went downstairs, out to his car. The engine turned over as soon as he switched on and his car accelerated smoothly into the traffic flow outside the square. He crossed the river by Vauxhall Bridge and bore round the Oval, past Clapham Common; by timing the traffic lights he got a near-continuous flow of greens through Balham and Tooting.

He turned off Marton High Street and threaded a way through back streets, found a parking space. Across the street, sunlight starkly revealed the front of a house that had seen better days. Once it might have housed a large family and servants; now it was obviously split into flats. A uniformed constable stood squarely in the doorway.

'Yes sir?'

'My name's Shield. If Chief Inspector Emery's here, perhaps you'd let him know I've arrived.'

The constable retreated to the foot of the stairs and called up, Emery's voice came back faintly.

'Okay sir. You can go up.'

Shield climbed carpeted stairs to an open doorway. Inside, detectives milled about and, standing like a rock in the centre, Chief Inspector Emery waited impatiently for results. He turned, jabbing with a smouldering briar.

'Hello, Dan, you might as well come in as you're here. Think you're going to find the missing perfume here?'

Shield stared round the flat, watching Emery's men tear the place apart. 'Not if you haven't found it already.'

'Not even interested.'

'How's it going?'

'Slowly . . . too damned slowly.' Emery had a temper as fiery as his hair. 'Not so much as a suspect unless you count Grevil.'

'And do you?'

'I've nothing against him, except his manner. I don't like him.' Neither had Melody, Shield recalled. 'We're looking into him, naturally.'

'Seems unlikely he'd kill if it was his stuff that was stolen.'

'Unless he caught Cole at it — Maurice Cole, the dead man, a chemist employed by Grevil.'

'Are you sure Cole took it?'

'Looks that way at the moment.' Emery gestured with his pipe at the searching

24

detectives. 'We're trying to trace friends, enemies, relatives. A motive. A lead. Anything.'

It was a big room, part divided by a hanging curtain; bed and washbowl on one side, table, chair and a small gas stove on the other. Books and magazines lay everywhere.

'Cole seems to have been a bit of a nut,' Emery said. 'Atlantis, astrology, flying saucers, Esp — '

'Not too much of a nut to devise a new perfume; a valuable property according to Grevil.'

Emery made a face. 'Grevil cares only about his perfume. Cole worked twenty years for him, and he doesn't want to know. All he wants is his bloody perfume — that's why I shunted him on to you. Get him off my back. I kept telling him, this is a murder investigation — waste of breath.'

'You don't think the theft and murder are connected?'

'Coincidence if they're not — and I'm too old to believe coincidences don't happen. But we've nothing concrete to work on. The body was found early this morning, on the common near the windmill. Some kind of knife used, through the eye to the brain. We're still looking for the weapon.'

'Unusual,' Shield commented thoughtfully.

'Nasty.'

A file of letters, open, lay on the table and Shield glanced at the top one. Recent date. Headed *Stardate* and signed Jay-O.

'There's nothing there,' Emery said. 'The usual bumph. Surprising in a trained scientist. It appears he took this astrology stuff seriously.'

'So maybe we should.' Shield shuffled the letters, reading extracts, and his interest quickened.

'Cole was the solitary kind,' Emery said, knocking out his pipe. 'No close friends — just his job and these weird cult things. The people here knew him to nod to, and that's all.'

Shield was studying the last letter again; there was something in the way it was worded that made him think twice. 'Mind if I take these away?'

'Spotted something?'

'A possibility only. I'd like to get an expert to give an opinion.'

'Okay, Dan. Let me know if you find anything.'

'Of course.'

Daniel Shield replaced the letters in the file, tucked the file under his arm and went downstairs. Emery could be a prickly character, but he was a good friend. He got in his car with a satisfied feeling; it was just possible he'd been given the lead he needed.

* * *

Ryker's car moved in and out of the traffic with deceptive ease, heading south out of London. Despite blond, almost white hair, the man at the wheel was still young, his scarred face a mask of concentration. He wore a windcheater with blue-grey slacks and the hands on the wheel were large and powerful.

Competition racing in the GT class had given him a sure skill, but he always found London's traffic something of an ordeal. He reached South Wimbledon with a feeling of relief, parked, and sat a moment, relaxing. He lit a cheroot as he studied the factory building opposite.

High brick walls and a main gate, standing open; a side gate further along. A sign read:

GREVIL AROMATICS
Essential Oils — Perfumery Compounds

The front had recently had a coat of weatherproof paint; work sheds at the rear looked positively Victorian. The air carried a sweet smell of scent.

He got out of the car, threw away his half-smoked cheroot and went in through the main gate. There was a yard, with a glimpse of girls packing small boxes through the windows of one of the sheds. Inside the office block, he stopped by the receptionist.

'Mr. Grevil's expecting me. I'm from Ice.'

A blonde girl led him past a display of perfume bottles, along a passage to an office. Inside, a bald man in a check suit sat behind a desk, reading a newspaper.

'Name's Ryker,' he said amiably. 'Melody around?'

'She was — she's left now.' For some reason, Grevil appeared uneasy. 'I expected to see Shield.'

Barney Ryker nodded. 'I'm another partner — there's just the three of us, hire help when we need it. Dan's on the job, liaising with the police — that often pays off in our job.' Grevil didn't impress him; a small man, self-made. He decided there could be no harm in doing his hard-boiled act, letting his voice revert to its natural Australian twang. 'Anything new?'

'Nothing.' Grevil almost rung his hands. 'The police have been and gone and don't seem interested. I must get my perfume back — '

'Taken from here?'

'My desk drawer.' Grevil jerked it open and Ryker walked round the desk and looked down.

'Cops printed this?'

'Yes, yes. Cole's prints were on it.'

Ryker looked at the window, the door, knowing it was useless to comment;

people never thought about security until it was too late. 'Break in?'

'I trusted him . . . he had his own key. There are only two keys, and I have the second. Now he's dead and the Kyphi gone.'

'Kyphi?'

'The name we gave to the new perfume.'

Again Ryker got the impression Grevil was under some constraint. 'You made it here?'

'In the lab, I'll show you.'

Ryker followed Grevil outside, across the yard to a smallish newer building. Grevil opened the door with a key; the air was saturated with a sweet smell.

Inside was a workbench with more than a hundred small bottles, laid out in rows and neatly labelled. Along the wall were racks of large jars; Ryker noted the stainless-steel sink, a pair of scales.

'A finished perfume,' Grevil said, 'is a blending of many ingredients — essential oils from flowers and leaves, gums, animal scents like musk, synthetics. Only Cole knew the blending of the new perfume — it would be hopeless even to attempt to duplicate it without his knowledge. You see now why it's so important to get the vial back.'

Ryker didn't see. One scent was much like another to him. He asked bluntly: 'What makes this Kyphi important enough to kill for?'

Grevil's gaze seemed far away; he mumbled under his breath.

'What was that?'

'I left the office about six-thirty, locking up after me. Cole had left earlier. The police say he was killed between ten and eleven last night. So he must have returned and taken the vial between those times.'

'Yeah — ' Ryker stared round the lab; there was nothing for him here. 'Didn't Cole have an assistant?'

'He did have, but she left a few weeks back, and we haven't got a replacement yet. She wouldn't know anything.'

Maybe, and maybe not . . . Ryker said: 'I'll take a look at the common, see what the cops have found. We'll be in touch.'

He walked towards his car, guessing where Melody had gone; and convinced that Grevil was hiding something.

3

Puppet Master

'So Grevil is hiding something,' Shield said from behind his desk. 'That doesn't mean he killed Cole, Barney. It could be anything — there doesn't have to be a connection with the missing perfume.'

Ryker, standing at the window, watched the play of street lighting on plane trees in the square as an evening breeze gently stirred their leaves. His painter's eye noted a loss of colour, the subtlety of silver-grey tones . . .

Smoke swirled from his cheroot as he turned abruptly and paced back towards the oak desk, moccasins silent on deep blue carpeting.

'I still figure he's hiding something we should know, Dan. When I asked him what made a perfume worth killing for, he clammed up and switched the talk.'

'Melody may have something when she gets here.'

Ryker gestured at an open file of letters beneath the desk lamp. 'This astrology deal — you reckon there's anything to it?'

'I've phoned Chris and made an appointment for ten tomorrow. At home, so I'll be late in. And yes, it looks so to me, but I'll reserve judgment till he's had a chance to study these letters. I'd like you to run a preliminary check on Stardata.'

'Will do. There was no trace of the scent bottle, or murder weapon, on the common. Looks like a rendezvous and Cole bought it. No lead there.'

'Assuming Cole took the bottle with him and — ' Shield broke off as the office door opened.

Melody Gay, hand resting on the arm of a young girl, came through the doorway. 'Hello Barney, Dan — this is Ann Thomas, Cole's lab assistant.'

'Hi, Ann.' Ryker brought a chair for their visitor. 'Can I get you something? A drink? Cigarette?'

Ann Thomas looked uncertain, nervous as her gaze rested on Ryker's scarred face and white hair, travelled round the room, lingering on the chess problem set up on a corner table, the wall rack filled with reference books.

Shield rose, coming round his desk, hand outstretched. 'Nice of you to come, Miss Thomas. You may be able to help us.' He studied her as she perched tensely on the edge of the chair; budding figure, sharp features, casual clothes by C & A. 'Anything you can tell us about Maurice Cole will certainly help. His work, his friends, what sort of man he was — '

'I don't know who killed him.' Her voice held a cockney whine.

'We don't expect that — it's just a general impression we're after.'

'Well . . . he seemed harmless enough to me. Always wrapped up in his work. I only saw him at the lab, of course, but he didn't have any other interests that I heard of.'

'Interesting,' Shield commented, thinking; so Cole kept quiet about his astrology — afraid of the 'crank' label? Or just naturally secretive?

'He used to work late a lot — '

'When he worked late, was it on the new perfume?'

'I suppose so. He was always trying out different blendings. That was his job really, that and checking the production batches.'

'Were there many callers at the lab? Anyone who showed a more than usual interest in his work?'

'No, very few ... Grevil, of course. And an occasional salesman.'

Melody said: 'He tried out the new perfume on Ann.'

Ann Thomas stared silently at the carpet and Melody walked over to a filing cabinet and brought back a Riesling and glasses. She poured, handing the first glass to Ann.

'This'll make you feel better.'

Shield offered a king-size. 'Try to relax, Miss Thomas. We're all friends here and you can speak freely.'

'Grevil gave her a bad time,' Melody said.

Ann gulped half her wine and began to speak in a low voice, not looking at them. 'I knew what Grevil was like — couldn't keep his hands to himself. That didn't worry me, I was sure I could handle him. I still don't understand what happened, that's what terrifies me.' She looked up from the floor, and her voice sharpened. 'I'm not going near him again.'

Shield said firmly: 'You don't have to.'

'This was after using the perfume?' Melody coaxed.

'Yes, I was just putting on my coat to leave one night when Grevil came into the lab. Maurice was there and passed him the new perfume — it was in a funny bottle. Grevil said something about it being quite new and wanted me to be the first to try it.'

Ann Thomas paused. 'Something odd happened then. They both turned away from me and put their hands to their faces — I don't know if that means anything.'

Melody said: 'What did it smell like?'

'A sick smell. I didn't like it, but I wanted to get away so I dabbed some on. Just a dab it was — '

'Do you have any idea what went into the new scent?'

'No . . . ' Ann gulped the rest of her wine. 'I don't know how to put this. It didn't do anything obvious to me — I didn't feel any different — but when Grevil put his hands on me, I didn't object. I loathed him but didn't seem to have any willpower left. When he said I had to go with him, I went . . . to his flat.'

'Just like that?' Shield raised an eyebrow. Ryker stared at her in disbelief.

'Just like that,' she affirmed. 'I still can't understand how I gave in. It doesn't make sense — I seemed unable to resist.'

She ground her cigarette vigorously in the ashtray. 'I wish it was Grevil who got killed.'

'How long were you with him?'

'Three days . . . and I was kept in a room on my own most of the time. Then I found I didn't have to do what he said, and got out fast.'

'And you only used the perfume the one time?'

'Yes.'

Shield deliberated, then said: 'Thank you, Miss Thomas — Barney, perhaps you'll drive her home?'

'Sure.'

After Ann Thomas and Ryker had left, Shield rose and paced the room, his face hard with anger. 'If her story's true, we know now why this perfume is important enough to kill for. Something that saps willpower and increases suggestibility. What d'you think about it, Melody?'

'I think I'd like to feed Grevil to Suki ... there's nothing in the books on this kind of reaction.'

'A scent that turns people into puppets,' Shield said grimly. 'Who's got it now? And how does he intend to use it?'

★ ★ ★

The lounge of Shield's penthouse flat had been arranged to relax in; a big room with comfortable armchairs, books, records and paintings. The window framed a view across Regent's Park.

Shield rose late and ate his sausage and bacon beside the window, occasionally raising binoculars to watch the animals in the zoo. He was admiring the seals as they tirelessly crossed and re-crossed their pool, like flexible torpedoes, when the buzzer sounded. He placed the binoculars on the window shelf and went to the door, opened it to a young six-footer.

'Glad you could come, Chris — I'll brew fresh coffee.'

Chris Usher said: 'Nice of you to call me, Dan — I know you always have something interesting.'

'Make yourself at home.' Shield refilled the percolator and switched on.

Usher sprawled in an armchair, tossing his briefcase aside. He had a cherubic face and innocent blue eyes that masked an analytical brain; a physicist, he made a hobby of investigating psi phenomena, astrology and flying saucers. And, in his opinion, after deducting the fakes and natural explanations, there was something left science could not account for.

Shield passed him the file of letters he had taken from Cole's flat. 'I'd like an opinion on these, Chris. They're in sequence.'

Usher browsed through them. 'Stardata . . . heard of them, run by Jay Orbison. A big outfit now, based on Alderney, and working mainly with computerized horoscopes.'

Shield poured coffee and went back to watching the seals.

When Usher had read each letter through, he commented: 'There's something odd here, Dan,' and opened his briefcase and took out blank horoscope charts and a copy of Raphael's Ephemeris. For a time, he computed in silence, pausing only to finish his coffee.

'You know, Dan, sometimes you worry me. These letters could be perfectly innocent. The horoscope is cast correctly, and the interpretation accords with orthodox astrological principles. Naturally, each astrologer will give a personal slant to any reading . . . but I see what you're getting at. And I have to admit you could be right.'

'Let's say I've a suspicious mind, Chris. The letters are dated and they add up to something nasty. As you know, British Intelligence used something similar during World War Two — planting misleading information to fool the Nazis.'

Shield took back the file and went

through the letters, lightly underlining certain passages with a pencil. 'Can we agree that these are the ones that really count?'

Usher went through them again, concentrating on the passages Shield had emphasized:

'The stars foretell that a dream you have long held will come true this year . . .

'You are in a strong position. Decide what is important to you and put all your effort into achieving this . . .

'Next week, contact with a stranger may increase your prospects . . .

'A new friend will provide the opportunity of a lifetime. Accept his offer . . .

'Nothing can go wrong with your plans, providing you keep them to yourself . . . '

And the final letter: 'This is your moment of destiny. Do not hesitate to break routine — events are in your favour. Success can be yours, everything you've always wanted. Reach out and grasp your opportunity. Now.'

'Yes,' Usher said, 'it's well done. The

astrological detail is thorough, directing Cole's attention to a certain date that is particularly promising for — what, Dan?'

'Theft. And Cole wouldn't have been looking for that kind of trickery. He was a lonely man, he believed — he'd take it all at face value, take it step by step — '

'Was?'

'He's dead now. Murdered.'

In the silence that fell across the big room above Regent's Park, the trumpeting of an elephant could clearly be heard.

Usher looked upset. 'If it can be done once — '

Shield nodded. 'This is probably not the first time. Emery dismissed the letters as the usual bumph. So what we have is one of the oldest professions used by a modern industrial spy. And the victim dances like a puppet on a string.'

'I can find out more about Stardata for you,' Usher volunteered.

'I've got Barney digging into them, Chris. But they must have legitimate clients as a cover — can you get me the name of one? I'll need a name as reference when I go calling.'

'That shouldn't be too difficult, Dan. I think I've enough contacts in the field to dig out one name for you.'

'Treat it as urgent, please.'

★ ★ ★

When Shield walked into I:C:E's reception room, Ryker was saying: 'Spooky feeling . . . me taking a girl home and not knowing how to handle her!'

Melody, at the switchboard, looked interested. 'So how did you?'

'Strictly big brother.'

Shield shrugged out of his car coat. 'I assume it's Ann Thomas you're talking about. What d'you think of her story now?'

Ryker struck a match for his cheroot, puffed. 'It looks good — wary as a cat up a tree. I'll think twice before buying a girl a bottle of perfume again.'

'She'll get over it,' Melody said calmly.

'What have you got on Orbison?'

'Interesting type. Took a B.Sc., soon as he left University, switched to porno — pics as well as text — went to Spain to dodge the cops, later made his peace with the law. Seems to have picked up astrology from the gypsies and gone into business for himself. Operates from Alderney now, does computer horoscopes for the millions, and makes a bomb out of it.'

'That's not all he does,' Shield said. 'He also has a specialised service — do you think he believes in astrology himself?'

Ryker thought about it. 'Could be. The way I read him, he's the sort to convince himself he believes in what he's doing at any given moment. But listen to this . . . Orbison has his own private plane, and the night Cole was murdered he flew over here. I can't trace his movements from the airport, but the following morning he flew right back again. Just the one night, so — '

'The time checks,' Shield said, and gave them the gist of Usher's comment.

'This Orbison looks promising,' Melody said.

'So we'll take a look at his Alderney set-up. Book two seats on a morning flight, Melody.'

4

Thunderbird Two

The 09.30 flight from Southampton arrowed down above a choppy grey area studded with rock. The small island of Alderney loomed ahead of the aircraft, a bare cliff face rushing towards them.

As the wheels touched down on the airfield, uncomfortably close to the edge of the cliff, Melody let out her breath. 'That I wouldn't like in bad weather.'

Shield unfastened his seatbelt. 'If you lived here, you'd get used to it. The locals fly over to Guernsey to do their shopping.'

A salt-scented wind gusted in from the west as they climbed down from the plane.

Shield said: 'Remember, this is a tight little island, and there won't be much that doesn't get back to Orbison. Be careful how you put your questions.'

Leaving Melody to deal with their bags and hotel, he passed through the booking hall to a waiting taxi. 'Stardata House.'

The driver, young with a weathered face, nodded and drove off at a leisurely speed, left from the airport and away from the town of St. Anne, right down to Clonque Bay. Heathland spread out on either side, with sudden glimpses of craggy cliffs.

'It's a thriving business Jay-O has, sir,' the driver commented. 'Always a lot of visitors.'

Shield made a non-committal sound; tempted to follow up an obvious lead, he decided against it. He needed to keep his head clear if he were to assess Orbison. Besides, Melody had that job in hand.

Stardata was on the coast road, a modern building of concrete and glass, long and sprawling behind a high brick wall. The taxi swung in through a gateway; iron gates that would provide a solid barrier when locked.

There was a concrete parking lot in front of reception and Shield paid off his driver and went through into a hallway.

A girl looked up from her desk and smiled. 'You have an appointment, sir?'

'No, but I'd like to see Mr. Orbison. My name's Shield. Jay-O was recommended to me by Ted Wilmot.'

'One moment, sir.' As the receptionist used an intercom, Shield prayed that Wilmot's name — supplied by Chris Usher — would be acceptable.

After a brief dialogue, she said: 'If you'll take a seat, Mr. Shield, Jay-O will be down shortly.'

He sat in a padded leather chair, picked up a magazine and idly turned the pages as he studied his surroundings. Tiled floor like a giant chessboard, short flight of steps at one end, swing door at the other. The décor, like the receptionist, well-groomed.

A dapper man came down the stairs and across the hall. 'Mr. Shield? I'm Orbison.'

Shield rose, towering over the domed head and pink shirt. 'Glad you could find the time.' He found it impossible to read the eyes behind tinted lenses and wondered if that was the intention.

'Normally,' Orbison went on, 'I only see people by appointment. We're very busy here. But as you've taken the trouble to come, perhaps I can show you round.'

'That would be interesting,' Shield said mildly. And an obvious way to disarm suspicion.

'Our computer is through here.'

Shield followed through the swing door and along a passage.

'Our business is mainly in computer-ized horoscopes. But you'll want the personal touch, of course.'

'Of course. Ted Wilmot is very impressed by your reading. Accurate in every detail, he says.'

Orbison smiled. 'That's good to hear.'

Shield studied the computer as high-speed printers racketed. It was big and it was modern. Half the room was taken up by data-preparation girls; a large flow chart was pinned on a board above the programmer's console.

'Looks good,' he offered.

Orbison's gaze travelled over Shield's suit, assessing his potential. 'And what business are you in, Mr. Shield?'

'Intelligence.'

Orbison stiffened, forced a smile. 'You mean business intelligence?'

'Naturally,' Shield replied blandly.

'Can I offer you coffee?'

'That'll be fine.'

They moved back along the passage and up the stairs, thickly carpeted, to a small office where a girl in a silver wig and mini-skirt sat at a keyboard.

'Coffee please, Virgo.'

Orbison moved into an inner sanctum and Shield followed.

There were astrological charts on the wall, a full-length mirror. Another door — leading to Orbison's private quarters? The bay window framed a view over Fort Tourgia and the flowers on Garden Rocks.

Orbison sat at his desk, toying with a silver ballpoint. 'You'll want a personal reading, Mr. Shield? That takes time.' He pulled a pad towards him as Virgo brought coffee.

Shield sat down, wondering about her; was she only here for decoration? How much did the rest of the staff know?

Nothing he'd seen so far struck a wrong note; but the façade was too smooth and he wanted to crack it wide open.

'Your date of birth, please, and time if known.'

Shield sipped his coffee; now he had to be careful how much he revealed. It would be easy for the astrologer to slip in a loaded question.

He gave Orbison the details he'd asked for. Shield was a Scorpio.

'And your place of birth?'

'London.'

Orbison looked up from his pad, peering through tinted glasses. 'Have you been to any other astrologer?'

Shield shrugged easily. 'Only as a sort of joke, some amateur. It was Ted who convinced me there might be something to take seriously.'

'You should certainly take your stars seriously, Mr. Shield. I do. Will you require a regular monthly reading?'

'Perhaps. That could depend on your fee.'

'My charge for a regular personal reading is one hundred pounds. May I have your address?'

Shield gave his home address.

Orbison rose from his desk briskly. 'It's been a pleasure to meet you, Mr. Shield. I'll send a first reading as soon as I've cast your horoscope. Then you can decide whether or not you wish to continue.'

Shield went past Virgo and down the stairs, out through reception. He paused a moment to light a king-size and study the area. A concrete path ran round the block, inside the wall. There was another, smaller, building, without windows; what was inside that?

Was there a chance the scent bottle was still here? Or proof that Orbison dealt in industrial espionage?

He went out through the iron gate without looking back, heading down towards the harbour.

* * *

The water in the harbour was surprisingly clear; she could see the stones of a submerged breakwater. Out past the harbour, a grey sea lashed at crags of rock and broke into white spume. Behind her, grassy slopes rose sharply to St. Anne. The air was noisy with the cries of gannets.

The island was not much more than another rock sticking up in the Atlantic, Melody thought; it would be a bleak place in winter. She moved slowly along the quay, looking at fishing boats and sailing dinghies. The wind from the sea had bite.

She had got nothing at the airport; no V.I.Ps had flown in around the time Cole had been murdered. And it was obvious — she lived in a barge on the Thames and had sailing friends — there was nothing of interest now anchored in the harbour.

But Dan had been right about the island; it was a tight little community. Questioning had to be very casual not to arouse suspicion,

Further along the quay, a fisherman was inspecting lines and nets. He was a young man and Melody dawdled to give him time to look her over. She had deliberately put on an uplift bra with half-cups under a thin white sweater, and tight slacks. Without make-up, she looked younger than her years; innocent as the wind whipped at her hair.

The fisherman watched her approach, openly admiring.

She smiled at him. 'Is it always as breezy as this?'

He straightened, running line between strong brown fingers. 'This is nothing, miss. You wouldn't be walking along here with a wind blowing. Nice day for a sail though.'

Melody laughed, acknowledging the play. 'I don't think so. I'm only waiting for my boss.'

'Secretary, are you?' His tone suggested he didn't think highly of secretaries.

'Something like that,' Melody returned lightly as his gaze moved boldly over her sweater and down to her hips. He would have known plenty of holiday girls.

She moved closer. 'I suppose a lot of people come here nowadays?'

'Aye, we get all sorts come to the island, some of them a real laugh. Only last week we had a foreign boat in — lot of dark-skinned characters who stayed aboard and didn't mix. Mostly visitors bring money to the island, especially since Jay-O arrived.'

'Jay-O?'

'Mr. Orbison, he runs Stardata. Horoscopes like. Insists everybody call him Jay-O, real friendly he is.' The fisherman brooded. 'Gets some rum callers, Jay-O does. This foreign boat, big it was, a motoryacht, sort of converted M.T.B. — '

Melody turned to give him a profile, shoulders back. 'M.T.B.?'

'Motor-torpedo-boat. Nice lines, fast. I'd have given something to have seen over the *Isis*, reckon she'd be done up a treat below.'

Melody's memory turned over: *Isis* — *Kyphi* — could that be more than coincidence? She gave the young man an encouraging smile.

'Only the top man came ashore, and we saw little enough of him. With his bodyguard.'

'Bodyguard?' Melody's eyes opened wider.

'That's what they were, tough guys. Daft here, but where he comes from, who knows? Didn't think much of them

54

anyway — the big man was a hunchback, not nearly as pretty as you. How about that sail tonight? That's if you're staying over, nice by moonlight.'

'I'll think about it,' Melody said. 'Depends on my boss. 'Bye for now.'

She turned and walked back along the quay, towards the hotel where she had booked in earlier. It was a small place overlooking the harbour. She used the pay box to call the office.

Her own voice answered: 'This is a recording. After the signal, please leave your message. This is a recording . . . '

Melody waited, then said clearly: 'Barney, please check out the Motor Yacht '*Isis*'. I-S-I-S. She was moored at Alderney at the time that interests us. Possibly Egyptian registration. Owner a big hunchback.'

She went into the bar and ordered a Liebfraumilch, took it to a window seat. The bar was empty and she sat quietly, enjoying her wine and the view across the harbour, speculating about the fisherman — it might be fun to meet him tonight — and remembering the days before she'd met Dan.

They had not been good days, she knew now. There had never been a quiet moment just to sit and look at boats. It sickened her when she realized she had thought her previous life exciting and worth any risk. Shoplifting, picking pockets, always on the run, scared. She could admit that now, she never had then.

Dan had taken her out of that, given her back her self-respect. She remembered his anger at the way the Thomas girl had been used. That was typical of him. A man for all seasons . . .

He came in then, joined her for a pre-lunch drink. 'Anything?'

Melody recapped on *Isis* and her message to Barney.

Shield drank his wine in silence. 'I don't have your memory so I don't get the connection. Isis — Kyphi?'

'Both Egyptian. Isis, the goddess whose tears were believed to cause the seasonal flooding of the Nile. Kyphi, a perfume traditionally used by Cleopatra. What did you make of Orbison?'

Shield finished his wine, rose. 'Let's go

in to lunch — the fish should be fresh here and that's something to look forward to. Orbison's worth another visit. Tonight. After dark.'

★ ★ ★

'All quiet,' Melody murmured.

Shield moved silently out of his room and along the corridor to the head of the stairs. He wore dark slacks and sweater, soft moccasins. The hotel was in darkness.

He felt his way carefully down the stairs, went through the kitchen and eased the bolts on the back door. Outside, the yard was empty, except for shadows. Melody joined him and they moved off together.

Away from the hotel, Shield relaxed. 'A pity drinking hours here are so elastic — it's been a long wait.'

'I thought the bar would never empty.'

Stars glimmered in a sky filled with high scudding cloud. Waves slapped the harbour wall and the wind carried salt spray. They took the road up to Stardata, seeing no cars, passing lightless houses.

They walked briskly through the night until a light showed ahead.

'Night shift on the computer,' Shield commented.

The main gate was closed and locked. He went over the wall, leaving Melody to keep watch outside, and dropped into deep shadow. He straightened, listening.

Nothing moved. Check the outside building first, he decided. Except for the computer room, no light showed anywhere.

Soft-stepping on concrete between the wall and the main building, he circled it, thoughtful. No windows; one door and that locked. Taking a picklock from his pocket, he inserted it carefully into the keyhole, feeling for the tumblers. Spring steel caught and held, and he levered, exerting steady pressure. The bolt snapped back and he gently opened the door. It was dark inside and small sounds made him wary; he was wondering where he had come across the odd smell before blinding light hit him.

Orbison's voice came from behind the torch. 'I've a gun on you, Shield, so no sudden movements. Didn't expect me to be waiting, did you? Careless . . . it took only a phone call to check that Wilmot had never heard of you. Ice, aren't you? You're well-known in the trade. All right, move inside.'

Dazzled by the powerful torch, Shield had no choice. He stumbled through the doorway, into warm air, thinking: Orbison wouldn't know about Ice if he weren't in the industrial espionage racket.

Orbison closed the door and light came on automatically. Shield saw wire-netting and birds on perches; he was in an aviary.

'We're quite alone,' Orbison said conversationally, and Shield turned to look into the large bore of a .45 revolver. The muzzle lowered until it pointed at his stomach.

'This makes a large hole if you're thinking of trying anything,' Orbison chuckled. 'I cast a horoscope for you and part of it reads . . . 'Take no chances with your health today'.'

Orbison unfastened a wire-door and gestured with his gun. 'Inside.'

Shield saw a bolt on the outer door and

hoped Orbison had forgotten it. He measured the distance, tensed, then shrugged. He had no chance for the moment. He entered the cage with the birds.

The door swung shut behind him, and Orbison fastened it again. The birds remained still and silent, heads cocked, bright eyes watchful.

'They're called Thunderbirds,' Orbison said from outside the wire. 'Watch this.'

Shield looked sideways at the perching birds, about a dozen of them, dark blue-and-green feathers with long pointed beaks.

A shiny bead fell from the roof and a bird swooped, its wing-beat a small clap of thunder, snatching up the bead in its beak. A small bead, the size of an eye.

Shield froze as he suddenly understood how Maurice Cole had died. Emery's words echoed in his head: 'Some kind of a knife used, through the eye to the brain'.

'They're trained,' Orbison commented. 'Now I'm switching off the training mechanism.'

Light continued to shine on Shield's

unprotected face, illuminating his eyes; to a bird they would appear as no more than bright beads to be snatched out of his head. He darted a quick glance at Orbison; the gun still pointed at him but the astrologer's attention was all on the birds. The bolt on the outer door had been forgotten.

Shield lowered his head and closed his eyes, edging towards the wire door of the cage. He could hear Orbison's breathing close by.

'I can wait all night, Shield. Can you?'

He could do little except wait. Being forced to keep his eyes closed hampered effective action. Wire mesh prevented him reaching Orbison's gun-arm. He waited, listening for a flutter of wings. It grew uncomfortably warm in the aviary and bird smell choked him. Sweat trickled down from his armpits.

He slitted his eyes to watch the Thunderbirds on their perches; bright eyes stared back at him. Belatedly he realized why it was the astrologer always wore tinted glasses.

He faced away from the birds, eyes

tight shut. How long before Orbison grew impatient? He edged nearer the cage door.

'Stay where you are, Shield.'

He shifted weight from one foot to the other; never before had he felt quite so helpless. He risked a glimpse at Orbison, stared into the muzzle of the .45, closed his eyes again. He began to count, slowly . . .

Presently Orbison said, a snap in his voice: 'You're wasting time. Face about and open your eyes wide. Get it over with. Open them or I'll open your belly — and you'll take a long time to die that way. My birds are quicker.'

Shield turned slowly — then the door of the aviary crashed open and the light went out. He heard Orbison gasp as he wrenched open the cage, darted through and slammed it behind him.

The light came on again and he saw that Melody didn't need any help. Orbison lay writhing on the floor and she had his gun in her hand.

'What do we do with him, Dan?'

'Just watch him,' Shield answered. 'I

shan't be long.' He glanced back at the birds on their perches, showing signs of restlessness now. 'And thanks, Melody.'

He left the aviary and padded to the front door of the main building; it was closed but not locked. He slid into the reception hall; there was no one about and he went quickly up the carpeted stairs.

Orbison's office was empty; he closed the door behind him and switched on a light. He went through the inner door to the astrologer's flat. A double bed, un-occupied; Orbison wouldn't have wanted a witness around tonight. He searched methodically, taking his time; no scent bottle.

He went back to the office and searched amongst the files. Routine stuff, nothing incriminating.

He stood in the centre of the room, staring intently. There were no hiding places. Orbison was a very careful man. He went downstairs, avoiding the computer room, and out.

Inside the aviary, Orbison sat on the floor, his back to the cage door, his hands on his head. Melody stood well back, covering him with his own revolver. She had removed his glasses.

'All right,' Shield said. 'Where's the bottle you took from Cole?'

Orbison watched him with hating eyes, silent.

'Drop him over a cliff,' Melody suggested. 'Accidental death — he just happened to stumble in the dark.'

Shield saw Orbison stiffen and knew he could be scared. 'Why not? He murdered Cole and now I know how — but it wouldn't be an easy thing to prove in a court of law. I think you've got something, Melody. Let's take a walk, Jay-O.'

Orbison came off the floor fast and flung himself at the door. Shield caught him with a right, knocking him down again.

'Ready to talk now?'

Orbison licked blood from a broken lip.

Melody said flatly: 'Kill him, Dan — we can guess where the bottle is, anyway.'

'You can't,' Orbison mumbled. 'It's not here, and I'm the only one who can tell you where it is now.'

'It left here aboard the *Isis*,' Melody said. 'So there's nothing you can tell us.'

Shield watched hope die in Orbison's eyes and knew she'd hit the jackpot. 'And we can trace *Isis* without you.' He hauled the astrologer upright and thrust him into the birdcage, wired the door fast.

'Let him sweat,' he said, as they went out into the night, locking the aviary door after him.

5

Wake of the *Isis*

'We're playing in the big league now,' Barney Ryker said, 'and if we're not careful, we'll be in it out of our depth. Listen to this.' He leaned across his desk to push the playback button on the tape recorder.

Shield and Melody had caught an early morning flight to Southampton and driven straight back to London. They were holding a lunchtime conference in Barney's office over bottled beer and sandwiches.

'Al Hakim speaking. Is that really you, Barney?' The voice was deep, accented.

'Yeah.'

'You are in trouble, my friend, so naturally you call Al Hakim for help.'

'No trouble, cobber, just chasing information.'

'Information, is it?' The voice grew

66

wary. 'I'll help if I can, you know that.'

'Sure. What have you got on a motor yacht, *Isis*? I-S-I-S. Could be Egyptian registration. And a big hunchback to go with it.'

The response was immediate; a flood of pungent Arabic. Melody murmured, 'Sounds fascinating.'

Ryker grinned. 'I wouldn't translate for a lady, not even you.'

The tape ran on: 'If you have anything to do with *Isis*, or Suliman Kalif, you have trouble, Barney.'

'So you know something. Spell it out for me.'

'*Isis* is Kalif's private yacht, fast, a smuggler's craft. A crew quick with the knife or gun. As for the hunchback. Kalif . . . you have something I can use, perhaps?'

'Sorry, no. Just digging.'

'And under the stone you will find the Kalifs of this world. He is the biggest crook in Egypt I assure you; drugs, women, guns, you call it and he's handled it. He has an organization and — these days — political contacts that make him

67

very hard to touch. I advise extreme caution if you're going up against him.'

'D'you know where he is right now?'

'No, but I would be interested to learn. *Isis* sailed into the Med a week ago. She is not back yet. What is this, Barney?'

'I'll call you back when I know myself.'

Ryker switched off the tape and spread mustard thickly on a beef sandwich. The scar under his shock of white hair was brighter than usual.

'Al Hakim's no wilting flower. He's a captain of the police in Cairo and he's tough — a pal of mine from the old days when I operated there. If he says Kalif is bad medicine we'd better take the message to heart. Anyway, on the assumption that *Isis* is on her way home, I put through another call, to the harbour at Tripoli. She'd called there, refueled, and left. Heading east.'

'You've done well,' Shield said. 'Perhaps now we can fill in the sequence of events.'

As he marshaled his thoughts, his gaze traveled absently round Barney's office: a stack of mounted but unframed watercolours, the top one showing a superb view of sunset over the Great Barrier reef; pin-ups from *Playboy* next to coloured prints of GT racing cars.

'It must have gone something like this . . . Orbison learnt of Cole's discovery. We'll probably never know exactly how but, after all, that's his business. He hooked his fish with astrology bait. Kalif was in the market as a buyer . . . '

Shield's brown eyes reflected a hard glint. 'Why should Kalif want this stuff? Why, specifically, I mean . . . after Kalif arrived at Alderney aboard *Isis*, Orbison set up the kill, flew across with one of his trained birds. Exit Cole at the rendezvous on Wimbledon common. Orbison took the vial and flew back to Alderney, completed his deal with Kalif. Kalif would sail immediately, I think.'

'So what do we do now?' Melody asked.

'We assume the perfume is aboard *Isis* and due to arrive in Egypt shortly. Interpol won't act on our say-so without proof. In any case, Kalif would smuggle in a small bottle by some other route — plane or camel. Obviously he's got the organization for that.'

Ryker helped himself to another sandwich, applied more mustard. 'How's Grevil going to take this?'

Shield considered the question a moment. 'Yes, there's always Grevil . . . ' He reached for a phone and dialed.

'Ice here, I'd like to speak to Mr. Grevil. Grevil? No, I'm afraid we haven't recovered your perfume. We know where it's going. Egypt . . . Yes, Egypt. We can go after it for you, of course, but expenses will be high.'

Grevil's voice rattled the phone as he protested the extra expense. Then his manner changed. 'Naturally, I want it back, that's important. I'll put a cheque for expenses in the post today. Now make sure you deliver the goods.'

Smiling, Shield cradled the phone. 'We're still on the job then. Melody see to visas and a flight to Cairo. Barney, you'd better let Al Hakim know we're coming.'

Melody looked seriously at him. 'You'd have gone anyway, wouldn't you, Dan?

Because of Ann Thomas.'

'Yes. I don't like to think of that stuff even existing, never mind being in the wrong hands. But this way, we stay solvent.' Shield sighed as he rose to his feet. 'Now I'll have to talk to Emery, and I'm not looking forward to that. He'll be sure we've been holding out on him. As usual.'

★　★　★

The office of Chief Inspector Lewis Emery was a class, well-lighted place. The big windows on the thirteenth floor of the glass tower block — still known as New Scotland Yard — looked out across the roofs of Westminster.

Shield turned from watching the traffic on Broadway as Emery replaced the phone.

'My men are on their way to Orbison now.' The Chief Inspector's voice was tart. 'You should have given me a hint before this, Dan. In a murder investigation I can demand co-operation.'

'I kept hoping to turn up some

evidence,' Shield returned mildly. 'I don't see what you can do without it. I still don't.'

'I can put pressure on him.'

'Perhaps.' Shield considered the idea briefly, then shook his head. 'Not the right kind, and not enough — you're up to your neck in red tape. I was concerned about your wasting time on Grevil.'

'Nice of you.' Emery reached across his desk to a pipe rack, selected a bulldog pipe and rammed tobacco into the bowl.

'You really believe you can prove he trained a bird to kill? In a court of law?'

Emery had packed his tobacco too tight and had trouble drawing. 'It's — bloody — fantastic —

'And there's no law dealing specifically with industrial espionage.'

'In this case, there's been property stolen.'

'The bottle has changed hands, left the country.'

'An assumption.' Emery gave up on his pipe, and took a fresh one from the rack; this time he filled it carefully. 'Orbison won't get away with this astrology racket again. I'll hound him out of the country and set Interpol on him. One day he'll make a slip and we'll have him. Just now, I want to throw a scare into him.'

Emery relaxed, his pipe going well. 'Okay, Dan, I know you've a business to run . . .'

The phone rang and the Inspector answered it, his face turning bleak as he listened. 'He has, has he? Well, set the wheels rolling and keep me informed.'

As he lowered the phone, he looked at Shield.

'Orbison's flown, literally. His plane's missing.'

*　*　*

M.Y. *Isis*, a converted patrol boat, cruised at a steady forty-six knots through the Mediterranean, heading east. Thirty metres long, and driven by three gas turbines, she cut through the water like wire through a cheese.

The North African coastline made a horizon to starboard; Tripoli lay behind her and Alexandria was still some hours ahead. The sky was blue and cloudless, the sea without a ripple, the sun a circle of molten gold.

Suliman Kalif, wearing only a pair of faded khaki shorts, reclined in a canvas chair on deck, soaking up the sun; it felt good after the damp chill of Alderney. He smoked a cigar, body relaxed, mind chasing dreams.

He had the perfume. If the other members of the syndicate performed as well, the plan could go ahead. How long before it bore fruit? A month? Two?

Kalif contemplated a rosy future. He'd come a long way from a tiny village on the Upper Nile. He'd taken chances and won. Soon the past would be forever behind him. It was a good time to put the past behind him; approaching his fortieth birthday, there were moments when he didn't feel young any more. It was time to pull out, put himself beyond the law . . .

A crewman came from the radio room, unreeling a coil of wire. 'Ship-to-shore call, Suliman.'

He tossed the half-smoked cigar over

the side and took the receiver. 'Who's calling?'

The voice of Jay Orbison came through a crackle of static, edged with panic. 'It's gone wrong, Kalif. A man called Shield, from Ice, has blown it.'

Muscles took up tension. Stony eyes stared out to sea. 'Where are you speaking from?'

'Eire. I flew out in a hurry, dropped everything — '

'And now you expect me to hold your hand?'

'Shield's on to you. He knows about the perfume. He knows you've got it aboard *Isis*.'

And who told him, Kalif thought.

'He may follow you — '

Kalif gave a grunt of sound, half a laugh, half a sneer. 'What if he does?'

'Get him for me. Kill him. He's wrecked my organization and I'm on the run.'

'If he shows up in my territory I'll take care of him,' Kalif said in a cold voice, and handed the radio-telephone back to his crewman.

He sat motionless, watching the sea. No one could touch him here; it was too late for interception now. And if the man called Shield followed him to Egypt . . . well, on his home ground, he feared nothing and no one.

But the bottle of perfume was in his cabin. He turned his head and called to the steersman: 'Full ahead.'

This *Isis* surged forward as her three engines each notched up three-and-a-half thousand horsepower.

Suiiman Kalif rose to his feet, a monstrous figure with the lump on his back. He padded along the mahogany deck and went below, dropped his shorts and stepped into his private bathroom.

6

Mother of the World

Seen from the air, the river flows through a natural rift in limestone rocks. The city straddles a river that comes from the heart of Africa; it is at once the oldest city in the world and the largest in the continent.

A cosmopolitan city, a meeting place of Europe and Asia, Africa and Arabia; a primordial city, strategically placed at the tip of a fertile delta and surrounded by desert. A mixture of old and new, minarets and tower blocks, canals and diesels, pyramids and cinemas.

Twenty-five centuries under foreign rule, it harbours Arab and Turk, Christian and Jew, French and British. A city with a history of bloodshed and flood and famine, rich in ancient monuments

Misr, um al-dunya; Cairo, Mother of the World.

★　★　★

The customs hall of Cairo International Airport echoed with a babble of tongues. The air was hot and dry and reeked with a sour stale smell. Sand had piled up in corners the cleaners had missed.

Shield and Ryker stood back from the crowded counter, watching with interest as Melody wrangled with a customs official who wanted to open the large wicker basket she was trying to get through unopened.

'This,' Ryker murmured, 'could be amusing. It can't be every day a girl tries to smuggle a python in!'

A uniformed policeman approached and saluted them. 'One of you is perhaps Mr. Ryker?'

'That's me.'

'Al Hakim has arranged transport. If you will come this way, please.'

Shield gestured towards Melody. 'She's with us.'

The policeman gave a brief smile. 'I shall eliminate the trouble. That is my role.' He turned to the counter, rattled off

Arabic and picked up the basket. 'Follow.'

Shield, Ryker and Melody fell in with him as the crowd parted; they went outside to a cab rank and stowed their cases in a waiting police car.

Their driver slid behind the wheel. 'Now I take you to your hotel, The Nile-Fustat, that is correct?'

'Yeah,' Ryker said. 'I like the old town best, stayed there before.'

As the car swung out from the line of black-and-white taxis, a man with a camera moved smoothly towards a telephone booth.

Shield caught a glimpse of anti-aircraft guns against the airport skyline as the saloon car gathered speed and hurtled, siren blaring, along the dual carriageway towards the city. Sodium lights pushed back the gathering darkness, revealing palm trees and blocks of flats and the walls of villa gardens.

'Things have changed since my day,' Ryker commented. 'It was mostly desert out here then.'

Both Shield and Melody were seeing Egypt for the first time; the racecourse and Technical School, the modern suburb of New Heliopolis. Then the lights of Cairo gleamed ahead; mosques and minarets silhouetted by the glare of neons. The heat of the dying day carried exotic smells as the car turned south to old Cairo, past street corner stalls and bazaars to pull up before the Nile-Fustat Hotel.

A porter helped Shield and Ryker with their luggage.

'Al Hakim will call on you in one hour.' The policeman saluted and drove away.

The Nile-Fustat was not new, the furnishings old-fashioned, the gilt-paint chipped. Shield registered at the desk and they went upstairs to their rooms, soaked off the dust and changed into lightweight clothing.

Shield and Melody rendezvoused in Ryker's room, a big airy room with a double bed with brass knobs and red plush curtains.

'It doesn't take long to get organised when you know the ropes.' Ryker had a selection of glasses and bottled beer on a tray on the table.

Shield crossed to the open window and leaned on the balcony rail, staring out across the Cairo skyline. He looked down on flat roofs between the domes of mosques, roofs that were alive with people; he saw clotheslines and bamboo shelters, a chicken run, a woman cooking over a primus stove.

Ryker brought him a beer. 'The local brew — try it.'

Shield sipped cautiously, decided he could get to like it. As a knock sounded at the door, Ryker crossed and opened it.

'Barney, my old friend,' a deep voice boomed. 'It gives me pleasure to see you again.'

The man who came in had the build of a bull, square and hard and muscular. His skin was dark with a hint of gypsy blood in it. A big hooked nose and gold earrings gave him a piratical air. He wore a tropical grey suit, jacket open, white silk shirt and two-tone tie in blue.

Ryker said: 'Al Hakim — Dan Shield and Melody Gay.'

The Egyptian gripped Shield's hand firmly. 'Any friend of Barney's . . . ' He turned to Melody, lime-green dress contrasting with her red hair, and flamboyantly kissed her hand. 'Such beauty you bring to dazzle my eyes!'

Ryker poured Al Hakim a beer and they sat by the window, drinking while Shield put him in the picture.

The police captain looked questioningly at Ryker. 'All this is true?'

'Too right, mate.'

'It sounds — ' Al Hakim paused, selecting his choice of a word — 'fanciful.'

'You can say that again!'

'I can believe anything of Kalif, but what is it he plans to do with this perfume?' Al Hakim offered his cigarettes, fat and oval and gold-banded. 'This I must think on.'

'Perhaps it would help if you told us more about him,' Shield suggested.

'Suliman Kalif is a peasant, an intelligent peasant, from the upper Nile. A rabid nationalist — Egypt for the Egyptians. It is said that he milks Russian aid for his own purposes, and his purpose is power. A big man, physically, with big ideas. Ruthless, anyone who gets in his

82

way he crushes as you might crush a beetle.'

Al Hakim blew scented smoke and gestured across the lights of Cairo. 'He is back now, his yacht at Bulaq. Somewhere he is out there, in one of a hundred rat-holes. And if you find him he has an alibi, protection. It is impossible to pin anything on that one. I have tried and I will try again. As a policeman, it angers me that he should go free. Perhaps you can help? Provide the evidence of some crime and I will gladly make use of it.'

Ryker looked thoughtful. 'Frame him, you mean?'

'You can afford to take this business of the perfume more seriously than I, who have other worries. Doubtless another dozen crimes have been committed in the past hour . . . and something is brewing that I do not like. There is talk of a new religion — as if we do not have enough already!'

Al Hakim crushed out his cigarette. 'I suggest, Barney, that you make use of your old contacts — some of them are still around. And there is a girl at a nightclub, the *Blue Sphinx*. She is called Safia, and dances as Cleopatra. She is worth viewing, I assure you . . . my spies inform me she is close to Kalif.'

He rose and bowed to Melody, earrings jangling. 'Now I must return to duty. We shall meet again.'

★   ★   ★

Shield woke with the light of dawn shining in his eyes and the call of the *muezzin* ringing in his ears:

'*Allah al Akbar!* Allah is great and Mohammed is his Prophet!'

Street cries echoed as he shaved and dressed. He descended the stairs to the dining room and waited for Melody and Ryker to join him. They lingered over a fruit breakfast.

'I've been on the blower and fixed transport for you,' Ryker said. 'Pal of mine, Ahmed, runs a taxi service. I'll be rushing around renewing old contacts.'

After coffee, the Australian left and Shield lit a king-size and glanced round the room. A long room hung with red

84

damask, tables lined up with geometric precision, each with its own dazzling white cloth, silver and glassware. There didn't appear to be many people staying at the Nile-Fustat and only one was taking an interest in them. A middle-aged man with ruddy skin, stout and balding on top and wearing a business suit.

Catching Shield's eye, he smiled and ambled over. 'Name's Cowan.' His speech was American. 'You folks from back home? I'm from Boston. Tremonnt Street. You know it?'

'I've visited . . . but no, we're British.'

'Yeah?' Cowan consulted his watch. 'Got to get moving I guess. I'm in the tourist game, checking likely hotels.'

Shield thought: a perfect cover.

'Waal, maybe we can get together over a drink some time?'

'Why not?'

A waiter approached their table. 'Your taxi here, sir.'

Shield rose, nodded to Cowan and, with Melody, went outside. The sun blazed and the air was already hot. A car, ancient and rather battered, waited by the curb. The driver, in pressed white slacks and open-necked shirt, had a pockmarked face.

'Ahmed, sir — a pleasure to drive friends of Mr. Barney.'

'We want to visit Bulaq,' Shield said as he climbed in the back with Melody.

Ahmed turned down a side street where Arab boys noisily hammered out copper pans, grazed a barrow laden with fruit. *Fellahin* crowded round a fortune-teller. The sun glared off whitewashed walls and a smell of sewers wafted from the alleyways.

'Some pong,' Melody remarked. 'Reminds me a bit of the East End that used to be.'

The taxi reached the Nile and turned north along the embankment. The river glinted in bright sunlight and *feluccas* with patched sails moved lazily. They joined a stream of traffic heading past bridges and the island of Roda, the Nile Hilton and the Egyptian Museum.

Ahmed slowed as a forest of masts and cranes showed ahead.

'This will do,' Shield said. 'Wait for us here.'

Shield and Melody kept in the shade cast by tall warehouses as they walked for the sun was furnace-hot. The river at this point was wide and sluggish, the water tainted with yellow mud.

Bulaq, the river port for Cairo, was one of the toughest quarters in the city; a vast warren of slum dwellings stretched back from the quayside. Sacks of flour, being unloaded from barges, filled the air with a fine white dust. Dockers swarmed everywhere, loading and unloading ships of all kinds. Further on they came to a cluster of houseboats, then Shield said:

'There's the *Isis*.' Kalif's motor-yacht was moored at a jetty, apart from the other boats. She was long and sleek, her white hull blinding in brilliant sunshine. She looked fast and powerful. Shield noted the radar aerial and the fact that no obvious armament showed to the casual eye. A converted patrol boat.

There was one man on the bridge; a second at the head of the gangway. Both were powerful men with cruel faces and hostility in their eyes.

As they strolled past, Melody murmured: 'Visitors definitely not welcome. D'you fancy meeting that pair of villains on a dark night?'

'Not without advance warning.'

'I wonder where Kalif is right now? And the perfume?'

Shield shrugged. 'Could be anywhere.'

They turned back along the busy quay, passing *Isis* again, and Shield mentally photographed the two crewmen so he would know them again. They reached their taxi and Ahmed drove them back to their hotel.

'Later, sir?'

'I expect so. Barney'll be in touch.'

They entered the Nile-Fustat as Cowan came out. As they passed, he said in a Yankee drawl: 'Mr. Shield, I think you should know the Russians are taking an interest in you. You were followed this morning.'

7

The *Blue Sphinx*

After lunch — kebabs of mutton — served on wooden skewers followed by fresh fruit — they sat over coffee in the near-deserted dining room.

Ryker's eyes were bleak. 'What d'you reckon to this Cowan character, Dan? Is he on the level? Why should he tip us off? And how did the Russians get onto us?'

'He seemed serious,' Shield answered. 'Anyway, I'd like to check it out. Melody, it would be a good idea if you called back at the perfume bazaar to see if you can pick up any rumours. Barney, I want you to stay close to a phone — if there's any truth in this, go to ground.'

'Okay, Dan.'

Melody picked up her handbag. 'Now?'

'Give me time to get upstairs.'

Shield and Melody left the dining room

together; she to buy a street map at the hotel desk while Shield went to his room. From the window, he watched her descend the steps to the street, study her map and move casually away. Immediately, a man detached himself from a doorway and followed her; a squarely-built man, white-skinned, with close-cropped hair and wearing a blue serge suit. Shield recognised the type: Russian Security.

He went down and out, crossed to the opposite side of the street. Melody took her time, pausing to look in shop windows or consult her map, giving her shadow no excuse to lose her. She threaded a way through cobbled streets filled with wooden carts, vendors of sherbert and lemonade. She had a knack of picking crowded streets.

Shield, following directly behind the security man, stayed with the crowd and kept a sharp eye on the slim lime-green figure topped with red hair.

They passed through an alley where earthenware pots and straw mats were on sale. Eventually, Melody reached the bazaar of perfume sellers, a covered way lined with ancient walls and doors leading off. It was narrow and darker, the glare of sunlight filtered out by a dingy glass roof. A strong smell of perfumes rose in the heat.

Shield moved into deep shadows. Flies buzzed his face but he didn't wave them off, not wishing to risk drawing attention to himself. He saw Melody hesitate, then enter one of the doors inside the bazaar, and watched to see what her shadow would do. The Russian stepped into a café and made a phone call.

Shield waited patiently, dividing his attention between the café and the bazaar. When the security man returned and posted himself outside the entrance to the bazaar, Shield slipped into the café and used the phone himself. He got through to the Nile-Pustat and asked for Ryker's room.

'Our friend was right. You know what to do — contact us as you can.'

'Okay.'

Shield replaced the phone and waited just inside the café, watching the entrance to the bazaar and Melody's shadow. He waited for her to come out.

*　*　*

Melody stood in the bazaar of perfume sellers, gazing about her. Doorways opened off them on either side; the Arabic inscriptions above them meant nothing to her. The smell of many-mingled scents was almost overpowering. She took her time, waiting for her eyes to adjust to the dim twilight; waiting to make sure her shadow had her spotted. Dan would be somewhere in the background, even though she couldn't see him. She didn't expect to. He was an expert at tailing.

As she sauntered casually, she came to a door with a sign:

PERFUMES
English spoken
Suppliers to Paris, London, New York

She stepped inside the shop to find a shadowed room of dark red drapes with shelves lining the walls. Every shelf was stacked with small bottles. Automatically, she checked; no swan-shaped vial.

A curtain swished and a man came through from a back room; a tall man, dark, with a pencil-slim moustache. He bowed neatly.

'I can help, perhaps? Please be seated, English miss. You have come to the right place for I have everything you can wish. Scents, oils, essences.'

Melody perched on a small rickety chair beside a round table inlaid with an intricate design. The shopkeeper bustled about, chattering continuously, collecting glass bottles from the shelves.

'I can make an exclusive perfume to your requirements, very quick. You have only to ask. Your hand, please.'

He drew the stopper from a vial, dabbed scent on the back of her hand. A fragrance of crushed flowers filled the air. 'You like it?'

Melody wondered how close her shadow was, and lowered her voice. 'Yes, but . . . I hoped you might know of a scent that has the effect of a drug?'

The small Egyptian stared blankly at

her. 'A drug, miss?' Then he smiled, clicking white teeth together. 'To arouse your lover, perhaps? He is not as enthusiastic as you wish?'

'Not quite that,' Melody said coolly. 'What I had in mind was something to make him submissive.'

A small shrug, 'I regret not. Perfumes to arouse desire, yes. This other is not known.'

Melody opened her handbag. 'I'll take this, then.'

As she was leaving, the perfume seller bowing her out, he said: 'You will call again, yes? You are staying long in Cairo? I can enquire for you.'

'Blimey!' Melody did not often revert to her native Cockney. She could have kicked herself for missing anything so obvious; worried about her shadow, that's what it was.

The Egyptian was looking at her with a startled expression. 'Pardon, miss?'

'Keep your hair on, mate. I mean, yes. I'll call back later — and thanks.'

As she moved out of the bazaar, into blinding sunlight, Shield joined her. He said quietly: 'He's across the street. Don't look. He followed you from the hotel, and phoned somebody from the café. Any luck?'

'Nothing. But he's going to make enquiries.'

They strolled back to the Nile-Fustat, ignoring the shadow who still tagged along behind.

★　★　★

Barney Ryker lay on the bed in his hotel room, window open and shutters half-closed. Heat didn't bother him. He smoked a cheroot and took an occasional swallow from a glass of beer on the bedside table as he talked to himself; he was practising his Arabic, pleased that so much came back so easily. It was years since he'd been in Cairo . . .

After a stint for NATO as a military observer, he'd quit to travel. A bodyguard job for an Arabian tycoon took him to Egypt; he liked the place and stayed when the tycoon moved on.

The President had not yet succeeded in

cleaning out corruption from high places and crime was still rife. For a while he made a good living hi-jacking stolen goods and selling them on the black market.

Until one night he found himself face-to-face with an Egyptian police lieutenant; a man who could not be bribed but was prepared to make a deal.

Al Hakim had said in a mild voice: 'I have nothing against you putting thieves out of business but — 'The voice was no longer mild. ' — you only take the small fish. I want one of the big ones. If you will co-operate — '

Ryker co-operated. With inside information provided by Al Hakim, it had been simple to hijack Mr. Big's loot; some of the proceeds ended up in Ryker's pocket and Al Hakim got promotion. Afterwards, they'd gone on the town with a couple of girls the policeman knew.

Good days, Ryker reflected, blowing a smoke ring. But it had seemed sensible to move on to England. He'd got caught up in the motor-racing game and met Dan. Shield was looking for a partner who knew the East; he filled the bill.

The phone rang and Ryker rolled off the bed, padded across an oriental rug to answer it. He listened intently, spoke one word: 'Okay.'

He crushed out his cheroot and poured the last of his beer down the washbasin. His face was serious — Dan had confirmed that someone had tailed Melody — but his heart was light. Time to go to ground. He liked the idea; it would be like old times.

He studied his face in the mirror. Tanned enough to get by — not every Arab was dark-skinned — and his scar fading. He stripped and unzipped a travelling bag, lifted out a faded and striped *galabia*, heel-less sandals and turban. He dressed quickly, adjusting the turban to cover his white hair. He walked up and down before the mirror, subtly changing his normal stride.

Satisfied, Ryker let himself out, shuffled along the corridor and down the back-stairs to the street. He was soon lost in the noisy, colourful crowd.

* * *

Flashing neon lights spelled out Arabic script on each side of the wide boulevard as the police car sped north. Seated beside the driver, Al Hakim had lost some of his flamboyance; his gypsy face appeared sombre.

'Your news is disturbing, Mr. Shield. I must find out who this Russian is and what he thinks he's doing. In one respect only, Kalif and I think alike — Egypt is for Egyptians! I do not like Russian Security poaching on my territory.'

The car turned off the boulevard and filtered through a maze of alleys, darkened and cluttered with parked cars. They were, Shield estimated, somewhere behind Bulaq.

Out of the evening dusk, a blue neon glowed, tubes forming a sphinx.

Al Hakim handed Melody from the car and nodded dismissal to the driver. Inside the nightclub, beyond the foyer, a blue carpet led to an inner room crammed with tables, most of them full. The headwaiter conducted them to a reserved table near the stage, where a three-man band played and a fat Nubian woman performed a belly dance. Al Hakim pulled out a chair for Melody.

Drinks came. The police captain passed cigarettes round and glanced at his watch. 'This girl — Safia — is on next. A thousand pities that Barney has to miss her act.'

Shield said: 'It's better for one of us to be able to move about unobserved.'

'Of course.'

The Nubian finished her dance to wild applause and the curtain closed; a waiter brought fresh drinks. Shield surveyed the club; smoke hung in the air; a predominance of dark faces with only here and there a European. He looked for the man in blue serge but did not see him.

Trumpets blasted a fanfare. The curtain eased back with a long swish to reveal, onstage, a court of ancient Egypt with Cleopatra reclining on a canopied couch, handmaidens fanning her with ostrich feathers. An attendant bustled on and spoke. She smiled and answered.

A pause. To martial music, Antony entered, clad in war-cloak, hand on sword. The conqueror.

Cleopatra rose and Al Hakim gave a long sigh as he contemplated her figure, full and rounded beneath transparent silks. 'A beauty!'

As she approached Antony, the lighting changed subtly to suggest an enigma in the painted face. Then she began to dance.

Cleopatra's dance was rhythmic, to pipes and drums. She moved easily at first, hips swaying, silks swirling about shapely brown legs. Her body arched, breasts thrusting, as she backed away, enticing Antony after her. She smiled as he followed.

The music quickened, and so did her dance, but still it was graceful. She moved as if she had not a bone in her body, as sinuous as a snake.

'She's a pro,' Melody murmured. 'Very good.'

The drumbeat increased, the pipes shrilled. Faster she danced, and the faster the more openly erotic her movements became. Shield found himself getting excited; he could not take his eyes off her. Neither could Antony . . .

She shed one silk after another, revealing more of her naked body with each. Her torso writhed as if in ecstasy.

And as her dance reached its climax, the Roman was reduced from conqueror to abject slave. It ended with Antony at her feet, kneeling, imploring her favours. Haughtily, the Queen turned from him and exited into darkness to a clash of cymbals. The curtain fell across Antory, still on his knees.

Shield wiped his face and exchanged a look with Al Hakim. 'Some dancer!'

'Yes, very popular here. You understand the symbolism? Egypt rises above the West.'

Shield turned thoughtfully to Melody. 'And she is close to Kalif.'

Melody's green eyes gleamed with confidence. 'Easy!'

8

City of the Dead

A burning sun hazed jam-packed streets and alleys. Ryker was swept along on a floodtide of Arabs in *galabias*, baggy red pants and European-style suits. Wall-to-wall, the streets of Old Cairo were solid with people.

He wondered what was going on. At first he had been glad of the crowd and infiltrated to use it as cover. But the rapid build-up had taken him by surprise. It was no riot, he'd had experience of those. This crowd was silent, dark faces intent, moving with its own unknown purpose.

Carts and barrows were swept aside. Hemmed in, Ryker had no choice but to go with the tide and concentrate on preventing his ribs from being inadvertently crushed. There was no possible way to get clear. He'd never known such a crowd before; dense-packed, the pressure growing all the time, as if millions of Cairones — old and young, men and women — were determined to cram into the smallest space possible. There was no hint of violence.

He found himself carried, feet barely touching the ground, into an open space and the pressure let up enough for him to gulp air into his squeezed lungs. Those around him gave him no special attention; he had been accepted as one of them.

The multitude ground to a halt, swaying en masse. The sun blazed in a blue sky and Ryker felt sweat roll down his body. He waited, looking about him. A fountain played in the square before a large mosque with colonnades; the minaret soared thirty metres into the air.

He ignored his neighbours, staring straight ahead. The silence held an expectant quality.

Then a figure appeared on the balcony of the minaret and immediately the crowd began chanting:

'Azad! Azad, the Holy One!'

The lone figure atop the minaret

looked old, tough and stringy as a camel. The face was weathered by sun and wind and fierce eyes looked down from beneath the flowing burnous. He lifted a hand and silence came again.

The silence lasted as if the crowd had stopped breathing to hear his words:

'God is most great. I testify there is no God but Allah.'

The words rang clear as a bell; an impassioned bell.

'Brothers, I come to you from the desert to warn of an evil thing. There are heretics in the land, blasphemers who would overthrow Islam and bring back the old Gods — '

Ryker listened absently; he was beginning to wilt in the sun.

'I have come to preach the holy *jihad*, the duty to fight all unbelievers. Great strength is ours. Take the sword and slay the infidels wherever you find them. There is no God but Allah!'

For a long moment, the prophet Azad looked down at the people below; then he turned and disappeared inside the minaret. Slowly the crowd began to break up, no longer silent but talking with animation.

Ryker edged his way towards the backstreets of Old Cairo, remembering Al Hakim's worry over a new religion; it seemed that someone else was taking it seriously too. Azad's harangue had been brief — but to the point. All round him, Arabs talked of the *jihad*, the holy war. Al Hakim was right to worry.

He found a lemonade-seller and quenched his thirst. Then he set about the business of locating Suliman Kalif.

*   *   *

From the window of her hotel room, Melody watched Dan step out into the street and walk briskly away. She saw the Russian slip from a doorway opposite and move after him. Very soon, both vanished from sight.

She went down to the foyer where Suki's basket, the python coiled inside, stood beside a potted palm. She carried it outside and Ahmed's waiting taxi drove up quickly.

'The *Blue Sphinx*.'

'Yes miss.'

Ahmed drove up the *Shari el Qaar*, past Garden City, to Liberation Square. Melody ignored the passing parade of shops and boutiques; concentrated on getting into her role as a cabaret artiste. It was not the first time she'd used her act to keep close watch on some suspicious character in a night club — no one seemed to suspect a snake dancer.

Long before she had met Dan, she'd taken a temporary job as club hostess and been fascinated by the snake dancer. The dancer had not been popular, nobody in the club liked snakes. So when Melody had wanted to handle the big snake she was made welcome. She'd been pleasantly surprised to find the python dry and warm to touch, the dancer had shown her how to handle the seven-foot monster to avoid being suffocated when it coiled round her. Soon she was performing an act of her own . . .

Above Liberation Square, Ahmed threaded a passage through the dingy twisting alleys of Bulaq and stopped at the stage door of the *Blue Sphinx*.

The neon sign had been switched off and the doorman appeared to have deserted his post.

Melody lifted out Suki's basket and told Ahmed not to wait. The taxi continued down the street and turned a corner.

Melody went inside, past the doorkeeper's box-like office, and along a passage lined with dressing rooms. She came out in one of the wings. Tables were pushed back and a young girl mopped the floor; a morning audition was in progress.

The manager, heavy-set with crinkled grey hair, sprawled in a comfortable chair smoking a cigar and watching a pair of jugglers. When the jugglers had finished, he turned to look at her.

Melody opened her wicker basket, and lifted Suki out. 'I'm a snake dancer,' she said.

He nodded and blew cigar smoke.

Melody drew her dress up over her head and tossed it into a chair. She wore spangled briefs and a bra underneath. She kicked off her shoes and limbered up, allowing Suki to wind about her body.

The manager switched on a small tape recorder and pipe music played.

Melody swayed on her feet till she got the rhythm of the music, then began to dance. Hips swinging, breasts shaking, she handed the big python up her body and round her neck and down again. It was a long time since she'd done her act; she got a kick out of it and was carried away.

Faster she moved, Suki slithering and coiling about her hips and shoulders. The snake slid in loops through her hands as she weaved an intricate pattern of steps. The pipes shrilled faster.

When the music stopped, and she paused, sweating, she realised that someone else had been watching. Safia.

'Okay, okay,' the manager said, flourishing his cigar. 'You dance tonight, yes?'

'Yes,' Melody said, coiling Suki back into her basket.

Safia came over and stood behind her; she appeared fascinated by the big snake, but wary of it.

'It is very dangerous?'

'Not really — not if you handle her right. Like to try?'

Safia jumped back. 'No! No, thank you.'

Melody closed the lid of the basket and slipped on her shoes and dress. 'I need somewhere to stay,' she said casually. 'Somewhere cheap.'

Safia smiled. 'I have a big flat. It is too big, and lonely when Suliman is not there. You can stay with me if you like. Your snake will give him the big surprise. You come?'

Melody nodded. 'Thanks, I'll be glad to.'

*　*　*

Shield stood beside the open window of his room at the Nile-Fustat, smoking a king-size and watching the sunset and dusk drape a mantle over the city. Lights sparkled from distant tower blocks. The temperature began to fall.

He turned from the window, stubbed out his cigarette and changed into dark shirt and slacks; hesitated over a sweater

109

and decided to wear one. Nights could be chilly, even in Cairo.

It was time to turn the tables on the hidden watcher across the street; the Russian Security man had been replaced by an Arab, but someone had ordered the surveillance and the most likely person was Suliman Kalif. Shield intended to follow their shadow and hope for a lead to Kalif.

He would have liked a gun in his pocket, though he did not make a habit of carrying one. After the recent spate of hijackings, it was tricky getting a gun through customs, so until he obtained one locally he was unarmed.

He left the hotel and, keeping to the shaded side, walked quickly along the street. He wanted his watcher to feel sure he was heading for a rendezvous and made full use of the quarter's narrow alleys and winding streets. A glance in a window showed that the man had taken the bait; a tall Arab in a grey suit, bare-headed; his dark face eager as a vulture after prey.

Now Shield concentrated on losing

him. He passed swiftly through a bazaar where oil-lamps cast flickering shadows and turned a street corner. He ran to the next intersection and vaulted over a low wall, landing in an empty garden. He dropped flat, breathing slow and controlled.

Footsteps came hurrying, paused, then moved uncertainly away. As the steps began to fade, Shield rose and peered over the wall. He saw the Arab fading in the distance.

Cat-like, Shield swung over the wall and set off in pursuit. The Arab probed several likely alleys before he gave up the search, then set off at a brisk pace towards the outskirts of the city.

Shield followed, using all his skill as a tail to keep from being spotted. He had previously studied a map of Cairo and recognised landmarks; the Citadel perched on its rocky promontory, the Mokattam Hills towering above the city. A train clattered and racketed somewhere in the night.

As the street lamps were left behind the sky appeared darker, the stars brighter. Few people were about and Shield dropped further back. His quarry was just barely in sight, and increasing pace.

The Arab came to a stone wall with an iron gate and climbed over it. Beyond lay a broad dusty avenue, a network of streets and small houses. He moved down the centre of the avenue, a lone figure etched in moonlight.

Shield went over the gate, wondering why it should be padlocked. He kept to the shadow side of the avenue, following his man. City sounds had faded completely; the air was still and silent.

He was puzzled; this whole area appeared deserted for no obvious reason. No lights showed in any of the buildings and some were in poor condition. He had the eerie feeling he was moving through a ghost town; and that was unlikely in view of Cairo's drastic overcrowding. He ransacked his memory for the explanation from a guide book he'd read on the flight out.

It had to be one of the cemeteries. The City of the Dead. The buildings filling the vast empty area all round him were not houses for the living but tombs and mausoleums for the dead. He was truly alone with the Arab.

It seemed certain now that the man could only have come here to keep an appointment. Shield closed the gap between them. Sand from the desert coated the streets. Moonlight on the buildings cast black shadows.

Shield suppressed a feeling of unease as he pressed deeper into the City of the Dead. He passed domed mosques and miniature minarets, stone graves where dead bodies mouldered. The atmosphere of the place was beginning to give him the shivers.

Ahead, the Arab veered to one side and disappeared round the corner of a tomb. Shield took a parallel street and ran silently through the dust to the next corner, waited. His quarry did not appear.

He moved cautiously up the block. Somewhere near, the Arab must have entered one of the shuttered marble mausoleums. He stared intently at each building but saw no movement anywhere. He stopped and listened. No betraying sound came to him. Where had the man got to?

Shield advanced with infinite caution, one hand pressed to the wall, feeling carved arabesques,

There sounded a faint drawn-out *hiss-ss* and something metallic chipped the stone wall close to his head. Shield dropped flat, cursing silently; he knew now that he had been lured into a trap.

His hand groped in the dust and found a piece of broken masonry. He tossed it through the air. *Clink*.

Again the sibilant hissing. No gun flash to guide him. The Arab was using a compressed-air pistol — and Shield had no idea where he waited in hiding.

Bright moonlight flooded the open streets. He wriggled through ochre dust, keeping low and close to the wall, in deepest shadow. The hiss of a shot came again, ricochetted off stonework and ploughed a furrow in the sand. Shield felt for the missile, located it; a metal dart.

He got to his feet and ran to the corner of the building. He was limited to the shadow area — the marksman had him pinned down and still he wasn't sure where he was. It could only be a matter of time before he closed in for the kill. And Shield had no doubt about that; he had been deliberately lured here to be eliminated from the game.

If only cloud would cover the moon he would have a chance to make a break for it; but the night sky was clear and cloudless. He looked up at the roof — flat and exposed to the moon. No good.

Another dart pinged off the wall.

No hope of the police turning up. He felt along the wall, discovered a doorway. Inside? He would be trapped. The only hope was to get close enough to the Arab to tackle him with bare hands. He explored the door; wood, and rotten. He wrenched it open and stepped hurriedly to one side, waited.

Now, if the Arab thought he had gone inside . . .

He waited, tensed for action.

High up, red flame stabbed the darkness. Night silence erupted in a noisy reverberating explosion. A second gunshot came hard on the echo of the first.

Shield didn't wait. He dived round the corner and ran. Someone else was taking a hand. Someone with a high-powered rifle.

He didn't look back but ran as hard as he could for the outside wall of the cemetery and climbed over it. There was no sign of pursuit, but the bark of a rifle sounded once more. The Arab and the unknown were fighting it out.

Shield left them to it, jog-trotted till he reached the edge of the city. He found a taxi and drove back to the hotel with one thought starkly in mind: first thing in the morning he must get hold of a gun.

9

The Perfumed Corpse

Safia's penthouse flat was high up in a sun-washed tower block in the prosperous residential district of Heliopolis to the north-east of the city. They travelled by taxi, with Safia in a happy mood, stopping only once at a market.

As they crossed the foyer to a high-speed lift, a porter carrying Suki's basket, Melody said: 'This place looks pretty expensive to me.'

'I don't have to pay rent — Suliman owns the block. And you'll be my guest. It will be nice to have someone stay.'

Melody remembered the slums she'd seen in the old quarter and thought: who was it said crime doesn't pay?

She tipped the porter when they reached the flat. Inside, she looked round the lounge, large and air-conditioned, the modern façade contrasting well with

Persian rugs and antique furniture. There was a lacquered cabinet and carved soapstone and crystal vases. The divan was Moorish.

'Very nice.'

'Suliman is a rich business man,' Safia said. 'He owns the *Blue Sphinx* too, and has a yacht — I've been up the Nile in that.'

She slipped off her sleeveless jacket, revealing an hourglass figure in a sheer blouse and bright red trousers drawn in at the ankles. No taller than Melody, she had a dusty complexion and her face was delicately painted. She might have been an houri from the Mohammedan paradise.

She took pride in showing Melody around her flat; probably it was the first time she'd had the chance to show anyone how well she was doing. The kitchen was compact and stainless steel, the bathroom European; the bedroom contained a large comfortable double bed and a dressing table buried under cosmetics.

'I will make coffee,' Safia said. 'Please make yourself feel at home.'

Melody heard her singing in the kitchen as she inventoried the flat. Pictures of Cleopatra on the wall; large picture books about ancient Egypt; a biography of the Queen. A gold crown.

She tried the crown for weight in her hand and wondered: did Safia realize it was gold?

Safia giggled as she brought in a coffee tray. 'Suliman likes me to wear it when he's here. And I have to study the period — he makes me study hard for the part I dance.'

They sat on the divan, sipping coffee.

'It is nice to have company, Melody. So often Suliman is away on business. He has business interests everywhere, even outside Egypt. And I get bored on my own. When he came back from a recent trip, he spent only one night — one night! — with me, and I haven't seen him since. Men!'

'I know just what you mean.'

Safia brooded over the coffee cup. 'If he should arrive while you're here — '

'Don't worry, I'll discreetly disappear.'

'You mustn't mind his looks. He's so

119

big — and a hunchback. He can't help that, of course, but it does put people off. I feel sorry for him.'

She doesn't know, Melody decided; probably a lot younger than she looks, an innocent. Who am I to judge if she goes after a good time?

'It's different for girls in Europe,' Safia said. 'I've read about you. Here, freedom is a new thing . . . and I don't intend to spend my life in an office filling out forms. I want excitement. My parents disapprove of my dancing — that's where I met Suliman — they're old-fashioned.'

'I expect he buys you presents.'

'Oh, yes.' Safia was on her feet, opening a cabinet. 'Look!'

Melody looked at several pieces of jewellery. 'In my country, a man quite often gives a girl scent.'

Safia looked blank. 'Scent? But Egypt is famous for its perfumes. It is so cheap here.'

Melody rose, crossing the room to her wicker basket, changing the subject. 'It's time I fed Suki.'

She opened the parcel of dead rats

she'd bought in the market, and lifted the lid of the basket.

The python's head appeared, tongue flickering in and out. Coil after coil of the great mottled body left the basket and rippled across the rug.

Safia backed off, staring as if hypnotized, as Melody tossed the snake a rat. One gulp, and the rat vanished headfirst. Another, and another . . .

'Want to handle her now?' Melody asked. 'She'll be sleepy now she's fed.'

'I don't think I could,' Safia said in a small voice.

'It's knowing how to pick up a constrictor, how to handle her.' Melody demonstrated, the diamond-patterned body weaving. 'You keep your hands moving, avoiding the coils — '

The phone rang and Safia answered, speaking quick Arabic. When she replaced the receiver, she picked up her jacket and said in an excited tone: 'That was Suliman. I have to meet him right away. I shan't be dancing tonight.'

When she had gone, Melody took the cups into the kitchen and washed them.

Then she began a methodical search of the flat. With Suki loose she had no fear of interruption; the python was better than any gun.

There was no sign of a swan-shaped vial; nor of a violet coloured scent.

She stood in the centre of the lounge, turning slowly, looking round. She saw Suki exploring the crown of Cleopatra, the sculptures and antiques. She saw everything, and nothing.

At the back of her mind was the nagging doubt that she'd missed something. Something important.

⋆ ⋆ ⋆

'What you want, Mr. Barney, is a dirty trick.'

Ryker nodded. 'Yeah. What kind though?'

Both men fell silent, considering the range of possibilities. Omar the Nubian was an old contact of Ryker's, one who had worked for him when he'd made a living by hijacking stolen goods. And was now keen to add to his meagre pay.

They sat cross-legged on the flat roof of a carpet warehouse adjoining a hotel with a bowl between them. Fingers dipped into the stew and brought out pieces of goat's-meat.

Ryker looked just another Arab in *galabia* and turban. Omar, skeleton-thin and black as soot, wore the uniform of a hotel porter. They were isolated from the rest of the rooftop community by a line of washing. Around this was spread out the slums of Cairo, a warren of small villages open to the sky; rooftop homes of servants who worked in the hotels.

The city shimmered through waves of heated air. Desert a muted ochre, sky a wash of brightest cobalt. Uprights of minarets slashing the mazelike pattern of square roofs, swollen curves for domes. Deep black in the shadows against brilliant sunlit walls. Ryker's hand itched for the weight of a loaded paintbrush.

Omar said quietly, 'To get aboard *Isis*, it will be best to draw off the crew.'

'Sure. And keep them occupied elsewhere for half-an-hour. I'll need that long, at least, to search the ship.'

'I can get reliable man. Together we can seize the yacht for you.'

Ryker shook his head. 'No go. I don't want anything that obvious. Kalif's not to be sure anyone's been aboard — I want to keep him guessing.'

Omar's face split in a wide grin, white teeth gleaming in his black face. 'Like old times, Mr. Barney.'

'A dockside fight,' Ryker mused. 'That might do. Yeah, a riot. Figure you can get enough men to split into two gangs? Get a riot going, right next to *Isis*, threatening to damage her. At night.'

'No trouble. I know some fellows who like nothing better than a good fight.'

'I don't think the crew will use guns. Hakim would jump at the chance of an excuse to board her himself. No, they'll have to leave their posts to protect her, and join in. You should be able to pin 'em down long enough for a search.'

'Leave it to me,' Omar said.

'Okay. Set it up.'

The Nubian rose and padded softly away.

Ryker sat staring out across the city,

visualizing the picture he would one day paint.

* * *

Ahmed's pockmarked face had lost its normal cheerful expression as he took Suki's basket and stored it in the back of his battered taxi. He looked wary.

When Melody got in, he drove off quickly. It was immediately obvious to her that he was avoiding the main road to the city's centre; he used side roads where the lighting was poor and made unnecessary double-turns.

'What's happened?' she asked.

'Mr. Daniel, he said to take extra care, miss. Someone tried to shoot him last night.'

'He's all right?'

'Yes miss, he's okay, but said to be careful.'

Melody digested the news in silence as she was driven to her evening performance at the *Blue Sphinx*. 'And Barney?'

'No word from him, miss.'

She knew that someone had been

keeping an eye on them since their arrival in Cairo, and assumed it to be Kalif. Now it seemed a shooting war had started. She wondered why, and made up her mind about something.

'Ahmed, stop at the perfume bazaar first. I've a call to make.'

'Yes miss.'

The taxi turned again, pursuing a zigzag route through dark streets. Ahmed drove fast on sidelights, watching his rear mirror. They passed through a narrow alley between high curved walls, a small square where pottery was set on a barrow, shops that were still open.

Ahmed stopped in the street butting onto the bazaar of perfume sellers.

'Wait for me,' Melody said. 'I shan't be long. If there's any trouble, just turn Suki loose.'

Ahmed's expression plainly indicated he would prefer trouble.

Melody moved slowly, letting her eyes adjust to the poor light. She scanned the area carefully but no one seemed to be taking an undue interest in her. She moved into the bazaar.

It was hot under the covered way, hot with a baking heat that had built up all day. Oil lamps burned in some of the small shops. She avoided the patches of deep shadow.

She approached the shop where she'd bought perfume and noted that the door was ajar. No lights showed inside. She slipped through the door and stood listening. The smell of perfume was overpowering, as if a lot had been spilt. There was a buzz of flies.

Melody called softly: 'Anyone home?'

She waited in the dark, uneasy. Only the flies broke the silence.

She edged forward, fingers trailing the wall till she came to a table with a lamp on it. She struck a match and adjusted the wick, looked around.

Warm yellow light revealed the neat man who had been asking questions for her. He was no longer neat.

He sprawled on the carpet beside a broken perfume bottle. He was drenched in perfume. The jagged glass of the broken bottle had been used to rip open his throat and flies gathered on the congealed flood that had welled from the ugly gash.

If he had learnt anything, he wouldn't be telling. Melody turned away, feeling sick.

10

Vanished Houri

By the time Shield reached the bazaar of perfume sellers, the police were already in action. Cables trailed across the cobblestones and powerful floodlights blotted out the night. Uniformed men held back a curious crowd.

Shield waited till he caught Al Hakim's eye, and the police captain came over and escorted him through the cordon.

The Egyptian was like an angry bull, swarthy face flushed, earrings jangling noisily. 'She should have stayed here — '

Shield agreed. 'But she might learn something at the *Blue Sphinx*.'

'That won't do any good. Kalif would only give the order. If we identify the killer, he won't talk — and Kalif will have an alibi. It's a dead end.'

'Melody's staying with Safia,' Shield informed, 'I told her to stick close but, apparently, Safia left earlier to meet Kalif. She doesn't know where.'

Al Hakim stroked his hooked nose. 'Odd. He wouldn't use one of his own for an alibi, not Kalif. It'll be two or three V.I.Ps in a government ministry. That's his style.'

At the bazaar, police were routinely questioning other shopkeepers. They crossed to the doorway of the small shop and stared in; a photographer was taking shots of the body on the floor; another man was brushing dust on the broken bottle.

Al Hakim gave Shield a sidelong glance, 'You seem to have stirred up something but I'm not sure what. Did you obtain a gun?'

Earlier, he had provided a gun permit after Shield had told him of the ambush in the cemetery.

Shield patted his jacket pocket. 'A Luger.'

Al Hakim nodded approval. 'No sense in carrying a toy. A gun's meant to stop a man,' He looked down at the corpse, fly-covered and reeking of perfume. 'He was asking questions for you, about the perfume from England?'

Shield nodded.

'But he wouldn't be killed just for that — he wouldn't stand a chance of getting answers, not where Kalif's involved. So he was killed as a warning. Keep your nose out of my business, and it works . . . nobody saw anything, nobody heard anything, nobody's talking.'

Al Hakim brooded as he walked about the shop, lifting bottles, peering into corners. 'Your Melody is in danger. She ought not to have gone to the *Blue Sphinx*. Tell her to stay away from Safia.'

'No,' Shield said mildly. 'She can take care of herself.'

'The second man in the cemetery. The rifle puzzles me — an unusual weapon to carry. A Russian and an Arab taking turns at tailing. I would very much like to have the pair of them for questioning. Too many puzzles — and now murder.'

'Anything on Cowan?'

'No. I thought — like you — the C.I.A., but my contact with the Americans says 'nothing known'. And Barney, where is he?'

Ryker was aboard a light skiff, sailing down the Nile. The water was black, dotted here and there with reflected light from riverside restaurants. He kept out of the lighted areas, using his sculls only when absolutely necessary, allowing the current to carry him along.

He had started from the island of Gezira, helping himself to a skiff at the yacht club, working his way towards Bulaq on the opposite side of the river. He glimpsed the tall silhouettes of cranes, rusting barges and further on, a few houseboats. He aimed the skiff for the jetty where *Isis* was moored.

Kalif's motor-yacht showed up, ghost-white in the starlight. Only riding lights burned; the cabins were in darkness. As he drew nearer, he made out the long sleek lines of a patrol boat, a radar aerial, two shadowy figures patrolling on deck.

Ryker cautiously closed the gap, expertly judging current and distance. At the last moment, he unshipped sculls and grasped

132

the yacht's anchor chain as it passed overhead; the skiff swung into shades against
the hull and he tied up.

City sounds echoed faintly on the night
air, distant lights gleamed through the
darkness. He heard pacing steps on deck,
a brief exchange of Arabic. He sat
patiently waiting, undetected.

Time passed and presently there came
the noise of a scuffle on the quayside;
drunken voices, a curse, followed by a
blow. A man called for help. Other voices
joined in, jabbering excitedly; a fight
started.

Ryker stood up, balancing carefully,
and gripped the anchor chain ready to
board.

'Bullshit! Your mother was a goat, your
father — '

The voice ended in a wail. A brawl was
developing; heavy thuds sounded on the
hull of the *Isis*. The two guards moved to
the dockside rail, looking down, shouting.

Ryker went up the chain in long, steady
hauls. He raised his head cautiously to
deck level and peered across the gunwale.
He saw the deckhouse and, beyond, both

guards gesturing fiercely and shouting.

The fight appeared to have developed into a small riot with more men joining in. To protect the ship, Kalif's guards jumped onto the jetty, knives in hand.

'Ya salam! Miserable dogs, take your stinking — '

Ryker rolled onto the deck and padded softly into the main cabin, paused, listening; the yacht seemed to be empty.

Outside, clubs flailed and a man screamed. Ryker took a quick look; the yacht's guards were down, buried beneath tumbling figures, shrilling curses in Arabic. He grinned; Omar's friends were putting up a good performance, though it looked like it was getting out of hand.

He pulled a pencil torch from under his *galabia* and began a quick but methodical search, leaving no trace of his passage. Kalif went in for luxury; there was a cocktail cabinet, a small library, record player. A double bed in place of bunks, a bathroom. The cigars in the wooden box were Havanas.

Sounds of fighting came distantly through the ship's hull as he stood thinking. No vial, no perfume. Would Kalif have hidden it in another part of the vessel? He thought it unlikely; in view of its importance, Kalif would want it to hand. But he still searched anyway. When he was sure the vial was not aboard, he went upstairs and looked out on deck.

Tyres squealed as a police car raced up. There was a warning shout and the fight broke up, men fading into the gloom between warehouses. The two guards picked themselves up, bruised and bleeding. The police began to fire questions.

Ryker slithered across the deck to the far side and down the anchor chain. He cast off, and the current carried the skiff out into midstream. At a safe distance, he used the sculls and headed back to Gezira. With luck, if he could replace the skiff unobserved, no one would ever know he'd been aboard the *Isis*.

And after that? There was nothing else for it; Omar would have to recruit an army of spies to locate Kalif's hideout.

★   ★   ★

Ahmed's taxi was waiting outside the stage door of the *Blue Sphinx* when Melody came out. Because of Safia's absence, she'd been asked to perform her dance a second time. So it was in the early hours when she left the club.

The air was cool but did little to dispel the garbage-smell around the back exit.

Ahmed lifted Suki's basket into the cab. 'Heliopolis,' she said. 'Tell Dan I'll be staying there till Safia shows up.'

'Okay, miss.'

He drove out of Bulaq, taking the main road this time. Traffic was light and he built up speed, still watching the rear mirror.

Melody wasn't interested; she was thinking about Safia, wondering if she had returned yet. A casual enquiry at the nightclub had shown her the manager knew nothing. He'd grumbled a bit because the Cleopatra dance was a good draw — but he wasn't seriously concerned. Safia was Kalif's girl friend, and Kalif was the boss.

As the kilometres passed, Melody framed innocent questions for Safia, questions that might give her a lead to Kalif.

The taxi stopped outside the tower block and Melody went in. She had a key and went straight to the lift. The passage was quiet when she got out on the top floor, the light dimmed; there was only the penthouse this high. She opened the door. It was dark inside and she groped for the wall switch. Light came on and she halted abruptly in the doorway, staring at the lounge.

The room looked different. Very different.

Melody glanced back along the passage to make sure she was alone. Then she slipped into the flat, closed the door behind her and turned Suki loose.

The rugs and antiques, the lacquered cabinet and vases that had given the place an oriental lived-in look were gone — replaced by characterless modern stuff.

Melody went swiftly from room to room. No cosmetics in the bedroom, starched white sheets that had never been used. No toiletries in the bathroom. The kitchen as empty as Mrs. Hubbard's cupboard. No clothes.

The air conditioner hummed steadily, not quite killing the smell of polish. Now the penthouse was just another anonymous flat without a sign that Safia had ever lived there.

Melody stood in the centre of the lounge. No pictures of Cleopatra, no books on ancient Egypt. Someone had gone to an immense amount of trouble to remove all traces of Safia's residence.

She coiled Suki back in her basket and took the lift down to the foyer. At the desk, a night porter said politely:

'Yes, miss? Can I help?'

'Safia, the dancer. She had the penthouse — '

An eyebrow lifted on a dark face. 'Not known here, miss. Penthouse empty long time now — you take, yes?'

Melody turned away, feeling out of her depth. She found a call box and used the phone.

★   ★   ★

Shield sat beside the hotel window, shutters half-closed to reduce the glare of the morning sun. He wore lightweight slacks and short-sleeved shirt, open at the neck. There was a glass of *Stella* beer on the table and he held open a copy of the *Egyptian Gazette* in front of him.

For some while he had been watching the street and wondering at the absence of a tail. No one had followed Melody when she set off for the *Blue Sphinx*. He wondered why the watchers had been withdrawn.

His attention returned to the *Gazette*, the only Cairo newspaper printed in English. It carried the story of the murder in the perfume bazaar. He learnt nothing new, but enjoyed the style; breathless Victorian.

Turning pages he found a photograph of an elderly Arab. It was a strong face, weathered and stringy with fierce eyes. A caption read:

'Abul Azad, the much respected prophet of the desert tribes, is presently in Cairo. Many thousands of true believers gathered at the Mosque of Amr to hear him speak.

'He will speak again —'

The door opened and Melody came in, looking limp. Shield poured her a beer. She took the glass and drank it in one long draught.

'God, I needed that.' She flopped out on the bed, kicking off sandals and wriggling her toes.

'Nothing, Dan. Bloody nothing. Safia's gone without trace, it's that simple. The manager at the club just shrugged it off — dancers come, dancers go, he couldn't care less. Not that I think he knows anything. It's the most diabolical thing I ever came across, wiped out as if she never existed.'

Shield quoted, 'Softly and suddenly vanished away . . . but which one, Safia or Cleopatra?'

'Does it matter?'

'It could do. At the club, Cleopatra was just another cabaret act. It didn't mean anything more than that. But the set-up in her flat — tell me about that again.'

Melody closed her eyes, recalling: 'Pictures on the wall, reproductions of Cleopatra; a lot of picture books of ancient Egypt; biographies of the Queen;

a crown, and I'm sure it was gold, if only twelve carat. Kalif liked her to wear the crown, though Safia thought it a bit of a giggle. She had to study the part.'

'All for a cabaret act?' Shield rose, restless.

'I should never have let her out of my sight — '

'You weren't to know. An obsession or something more? She disappears, and every clue to her existence is destroyed.' Shield paced up and down the carpet, thinking of Ann Thomas. 'I don't like it. I don't like it at all.'

11

Syndicate

The room was a large square, thick-walled, with heavy curtains covering narrow windows. In the corner stood a small table inlaid with gold leaf directly beneath an electric chandelier. Light bathed the table and a glass vial in the shape of a swan containing a violet liquid.

Three comfortable chairs were grouped about the table, flanked by rugs and cushions and lacquered brass ashtrays. Suliman Kalif sprawled at ease in the largest chair, a cigar between thick lips.

Across from him sat a solid man, square-shouldered with cropped grey hair. His skin was pale, his long jaw wolfish, his eyes empty of expression. He sat stiffly upright, gripping a square crystal glass filled with vodka.

The Russian said: 'It is getting difficult now. There are not so many of my people left in Cairo, and I have no wish to become conspicuous.'

Kalif drew on his cigar till the ash glowed. 'It will not be for long, Sekov.'

The Russian gestured towards the vial on the table between them. 'This is the drug? How can I know it will work?'

'It has been tested. The scent operates as a hypnotic, inhibiting the forebrain. Under its influence, Safia will become dependent — a golem waiting for my orders which she will carry out automatically.'

'The effect on another person — at what range?'

'A few yards, enough for our purpose. And the effect lasts. I shall arrange a demonstration.'

'Here?'

'Yes, when Fabian arrives. There is no point in setting up a second demonstration. Have patience, my friend.'

Sekov appeared not to notice the irony. Kalif was a nationalist; he might use the Russian, but no more.

'And you consider Fabian reliable?'

'Don't underestimate him, Sekov. The

idea was originally his. I added the perfume — and all he wants is recognition.'

'A strange man.'

'The English are strange. But sometimes useful.'

Sekov finished his vodka and set down the empty glass with a scowl. 'This man Shield is English. I would still like to know who came to his aid in the City of the Dead.'

'Does it matter now?' Kalif crushed out the butt of his Havana. 'I have Safia isolated, so the redhead cannot get at her. And we are ready to move.'

'That is so.' Curious, Sekov picked up the vial and held it to the light, taking care not to loosen the stopper.

Kalif's moon-face moved in a smile. 'Simple window dressing,' he said. 'A precaution in case Shield got close. It contains only coloured water.'

★ ★ ★

Phil Fabian drove out of Cairo, taking the road to the pyramids. He drove a hired car, slowly and carefully, aware that the aroma of whisky lingered on his breath. He couldn't cut it right out; he needed the stuff.

He was a gaunt man, knobby bone jutting under loose folds of skin burnt dark by years spent in the sun. He wore a faded safari jacket and khaki slacks that were short for his legs.

Beyond the built-up area, the wide road stretched away before his headlights, isolated houses on each side. As houses became scarcer, the desert encroached on the highway, and sprayed out from beneath humming tyres. There was little traffic.

He whistled an out-of-date dance tune . . . soon he would be respected. Under the new regime he would be an accredited Egyptologist. Kalif might get rid of the Russian, but there was no reason to get rid of him. He was only an archaeologist . . .

Once, Fabian had been a bright-eyed enthusiast. But enthusiasm waned as dig after dig produced nothing to make his name. He was a working archaeologist and needed backing. To get backing he needed a find.

The brightness in his eyes had faded from years in the sun, a continuing run of bad luck and too much whisky. If he hadn't been drunk at the time, he'd have known he couldn't get away with it. He'd salted a find — and, of course, been found out. Now no one wanted to know him.

He laughed, and the sound was bitter. He was going to get what he wanted.

He slowed as a track showed ahead, branching off from the main road. He switched off the headlamps as he followed the track to a house screened by trees. A low house behind high walls, almost unnoticeable; no lights showed from the house.

He stopped at an iron-studded gate, got out and rang the bell. A Judas-hole opened and a servant studied his face. When the gate was unlocked, Fabian drove into the courtyard; the gate was locked and barred behind him.

He remembered the step up to the front door and didn't stumble. Inside, the servant shut the door and a light came on. He went through the hall and along a passage, past potted plants, to the room where Kalif and Sekov waited.

* * *

Kalif sniffed indelicately as Fabian sat down in the empty chair.

Sekov said harshly: 'If you keep drinking, you will spoil everything. Just one slip, that's all it will take.'

Fabian's temper, never on a tight rein, surfaced. 'I can hold my liquor — can you hold your tongue?'

Sekov's wolfish face flushed but before he could answer, Kalif slapped the flat of a big hand on the tabletop. 'Stop it! I will not have petty squabbling. Phil, is the temple ready?'

'It's ready.'

'Good. Well, now that you are here, I can proceed with the demonstration. Our Russian friend seems to doubt my word concerning the effectiveness of the drug. This way.'

He rose, towering above the other two,

and led the way along a passage to a door. Opening this, he switched on a light and descended a short flight of steps to a windowless and barely furnished cellar.

He brought a flat tin from his jacket pocket and opened it to hand round small white plugs. 'It will be as well to fit these now.'

They took two each and, following Kalif's example, inserted a filter into each nostril.

'Wait here,' Kalif said, 'while I bring the girl.'

Upstairs he went to his bathroom and opened a medicine cupboard. From among a miscellaneous assortment of tins and tubes and packages, he picked out a dark green bottle with a 'poison' label. Who would look for it there? he thought, slipping the bottle in his pocket.

He pushed open the door of the bedroom. 'Are you ready?'

Safia put down a book and adjusted the gold crown on her head. Her dark hair came down over a diaphanous thigh-length shift.

'Yes, Suliman. Your friends are waiting?'

'They're waiting,' Kalif agreed. 'It's to be a small private demonstration.'

She followed him down to the cellar, smiled at the two men there.

Fabian stared back, disgust on his skull-face. 'I wish you'd get things right — this isn't a Hollywood production. She'd wear royal robes and the Double Diadem.'

'She will,' Kalif said. He took the green bottle from his pocket and handed it to Safia. 'Ignore the label. It's a new perfume I want you to wear.'

As she removed the stopper, Sekov and Fabian watched intently.

'It doesn't smell very nice.'

Obediently she dabbed two spots of perfume behind her ears and replaced the stopper. Kalif took the bottle, made sure the stopper was tight and carefully put it away.

'Shall I begin?' Safia asked. 'There's no music.'

'Begin,' Kalif said quietly, waiting.

She took a few steps, faltered. Her eyes glazed, her face took on a dreamy

149

expression. She stood immobile, muscles slack.

Kalif stood in front of her, boomed: 'You are Cleopatra, Queen of the Two Lands. You are Isis reincarnated, a goddess!'

The girl's bearing changed, became regal. It was as if she had a different personality.

'Who are you?'

'Queen of Upper and Lower Egypt.' There was arrogant pride in her voice.

Satisfied, Kalif pressed a button. An Arab servant appeared, looking expectantly at him.

Kalif said nothing. He watched his servant sniff the air; apparently the scent was a strong one. Gradually the servant's body went loose; his eyes misted and the muscles of his face relaxed.

Kalif said: 'Queen, your slave is in attendance.'

Cleopatra turned and faced the Arab. Her tone was lofty as she commanded: 'In my presence, you will kneel. Let your head touch the ground I walk on.'

The servant dropped to his knees, forearms flat on the floor, head banging the carpet. He stayed kneeling. Cleopatra's gaze remained fixed and distant, as if the slave no longer existed.

'Queen of queens,' Kalif murmured, 'your slave brings bad news.'

Cleopatra's eyes flashed. 'Then he must die!'

Kalif turned to Sekov. 'Are you satisfied now?'

Slowly, almost reluctantly it seemed, the Russian nodded.

'Then let us retire.' Kalif waved the two men towards the stairs. 'Cleopatra, you will remain. Your slave will also stay here.'

He went up the stairs, carefully locking the door at the top. Back in the square room, they took out their filter plugs and sat round the table. Kalif lit a fresh cigar.

'When the effect of the scent fades, I shall dispose of the man.'

Sekov poured himself a vodka and looked thoughtful. Only Fabian had a sour expression as he glared at the whisky on the side-table; he knew better than to ask for one.

Kalif drew on his Havana till he had the tip glowing. 'Safia will remain completely isolated until we need her.'

'I trust the final performance will have more build-up,' Sekov said mildly.

'Of course it will,' Fabian snapped. 'I'll be coaching her.'

The Russian nodded. 'And when do we start?'

'Soon,' Kalif said, 'very soon now. First I shall lure the hounds off the trail.' He picked up the swan-shaped vial. 'This I shall take with me, aboard *Isis* as I cruise up the Nile. Anyone interested may follow.' He paused. 'It will give me the chance to eliminate them. Then it will be your turn, Sekov.'

'Everything is prepared. I have a man I can rely on — and the use of a hovercraft. It is a Russian hovercraft, used by our oil prospectors.'

'That will make excellent cover,' Kalif said. 'Nobody will bother you in that.'

Fabian said: 'Azad?'

Kalif looked at him. 'Yes, Azad.'

Abruptly, Sekov swallowed his vodka and rose from his chair. 'I will leave now. There are details to arrange.'

The Cleopatra Syndicate adjourned.

12

The Prophet of Deir

'I am bloody annoyed,' Al Hakim stated flatly.

He stood by the window in Shield's room at the Nile-Fustat, inhaling on a fat oval cigarette and breathing out hard through his hooked nose.

'I'm not surprised,' Shield said. 'Surely it's a bit unusual, taking you off a murder case? Help yourself to another beer if you want.'

Al Hakim nodded fiercely, crossed to the table and wrenched the cap off a bottle. He was hardly able to contain his anger. 'It's never happened to me before. Pulled off a major crime . . . to act as nursemaid.' He almost spat. 'If I were sure Kalif has been pulling strings, I'd resign.'

Melody, in slacks and shirt, curled up on a cushion on the floor, asked: 'Azad is important?'

'Oh yes, he's important. A prophet from the oasis of Deir, to the south. That's what confuses me . . . but it would be a political thing and I'm just a cop.'

Shield glanced down at the pocket chess set on the bed beside him and moved a piece. 'Tell us about Azad,' he suggested. 'It might help set your thoughts in order.'

'Abul Azad is old, I don't know how old — he was well-known when I was a boy — and tough. A Bedouin, a nomad. He was what you would call a bandit chief. I met him just the once and was impressed, tall and fierce with burning eyes. This was before he was inspired. For many years now he has lived almost as a hermit, in the small oasis in the desert. He is highly respected, one of Islam's Holy men, with a huge following.'

The police captain gulped down his beer.

'He speaks and others follow. There are other prophets — but Azad is a leader, a warrior. And he preaches *Jihad*, and a Holy war is one thing we can do without.'

Shield said, 'Then perhaps it's important you keep an eye on him.'

'If anything should happen to him here, in Cairo, there would be trouble. Riots, disturbances, at the very least. I mentioned before a new religion . . . it seems to have started in a village near Deir. The local cops are worried, but what can they do? Now Azad is speaking out against it and his word carries weight. He could incite his followers to — well — civil war.'

Al Hakim looked unhappy.

'My orders are to see that nothing happens to him — and to see he doesn't start his *Jihad*. How, I ask you?'

'A thankless job,' Shield reflected. 'But an important one. So perhaps Kalif has nothing to do with your being taken off the case.'

'Perhaps,' Al Hakim admitted grudgingly.

Melody reached for a copy of the *Gazette*. 'I see here that Azad's due to speak again.'

'Yes, and I have to be there.' Scowling, Al Hakim chain-lit a fresh cigarette. 'If I thought Kalif was back of this — ' He bared his teeth. 'I don't know. Instinct tells me something is wrong . . . you have not heard from Barney yet?'

'Not yet.'

'I saw Safia's parents, they know nothing. There is no lead to the man who was killed in the perfume bazaar. No trace of your shadows — '

Melody said, 'I feel bad about that little perfume-seller. If I hadn't — '

Al Hakim turned on her. 'You must not blame yourself. It is Kalif who gives the orders,' He stubbed out his cigarette in a lacquered bowl. 'I must be going now. Excuse me, please, for pouring out my troubles like this.'

'That's what friends are for,' Shield said mildly.

Al Hakim bowed to Melody. 'When we meet again, I shall hope to be in better humour.' He looked at Shield. 'It seems I must leave Kalif to you.'

'We'll keep after him.'

'It worries me . . . it is not like Kalif to stay under cover for so long. I wonder what it is he's up to?'

★   ★   ★

Ryker sat cross-legged, his back against a low parapet, staring across the rooftops. The low mutter of Arabic in the background did not bother him, a husband complaining about his wife. A line of washing acted as an awning to shade him from the direct rays of the sun.

His gaze quartered the city; a network of mosques and shops, cemeteries and blocks of flats, hotels and gardens. There were a thousand hiding places as he knew from experience. All the same, Kalif had done a real job of going to ground; not one of the boys employed by Omar had caught a glimpse of him. Yet. Somewhere, sometime, a sharp eye would find him.

Ryker wondered why Kalif should bother to hide himself so completely.

It was a question of time, he told himself, watching the cars crawl along the boulevards, triangular sails of *feluccas* pass under a Nile bridge. He sat chewing a clove, waiting . . .

Omar the Nubian came hurrying across the roof, squatted down beside him. 'Mr. Barney, Kalif is at Bulaq. He has gone aboard his yacht.'

157

'Has he now? Sounds as if he might be going where the action is.' Ryker spat out his clove and rose casually. 'Good work, Omar. See that boy gets a bonus. I'll drift along and keep an eye on him.'

Omar's black face split in a grin. 'Sure thing, Mr. Barney.'

Ryker moved across the flat roof, flinching as the glare of the sun hit him. He ducked down through a hole in the roof, into shade, and made his way down wooden stairs to street level and out.

As he headed for Bulaq, he watched his back. Although he was pretty sure no-one had him spotted, there was no sense in taking chances.

He reached the docks where cranes swung heavy bales and crates aboard barges, moved between lorries and mixed with a group of workmen as he approached the jetty where *Isis* lay moored.

He found shade beneath a warehouse and studied the man on the yacht's bridge, recognising him from Hakim's description. A giant of a man, well over six feet high, hump-backed and wearing

158

khaki battle-dress. Ryker summed him up swiftly; a dangerous man, not one to tangle with at close-quarters.

Kalif gestured as he barked orders and men scurried like mice to load stores aboard.

Definitely going someplace, Ryker decided. He turned away, found a café and made a phone call.

* * *

When the phone rang, Shield scooped up the receiver.

Ryker's voice came through: 'Our friend is out in the open. Looks as though he might be taking a trip upriver. I'm at Bulaq.'

'We'll see you there,' Shield said and cradled the phone.

He knotted a tie loosely, put on his jacket and checked the Luger before sliding it into his pocket. He went along the passage and tapped on the door of Melody's room. She opened the door in bare feet.

'Barney's picked up the trail.'

159

'Two minutes,' she said.

They went down together, out through the foyer to the street. Ahmed's taxi was parked on the corner. Shield waved, and he drove up, grinning.

'Bulaq, Ahmed — and follow the river please.'

'Yes sir, Mr. Daniel.'

Ahmed cut through backstreets to the Embankment and turned north, moving fast through traffic, past the island of Roda and Garden City. Shield watched the river for any sign of the white motor yacht. They reached Bulaq without seeing it.

'Wait for us,' he told Ahmed.

With Melody, he crossed the dockside, passing cranes and barges, the air thick with dust. Garbage floated on the water lapping about houseboats; over-ripe smells assailed his nose. They came to the jetty where *Isis* had been moored.

'There,' Melody said. 'She's leaving — '

Shield gripped her arm and led her into deep shadow between sheds. They stood watching the sleek and powerful ship pick up speed, heading into the middle of the river.

'So that's Kalif,' Melody said. 'A big brute.'

Shield stared thoughtfully at the huge figure on the bridge.

'Yes, an ugly customer.' He watched till *Isis* became a dazzling white speck on the water. 'Well, we know he's aboard, and that yacht can't be hidden so easily. Nor will Kalif outside Cairo.'

'But has he got Cole's perfume aboard?'

From the gloom behind them, a figure in a striped *galabia* and turban emerged. It whined, 'Baksheesh, effendi?'

Shield was dipping his hand in his pocket when Melody giggled. 'Cut it out, Barney!'

'What's the plan now, Dan?'

Shield deliberated. 'What's upriver?'

'Asyut, Luxor, Aswan.'

'I'd like to take a plane and get ahead of Kalif — is that possible?'

'Yeah,' Ryker said. 'There are regular flights to Luxor. You can set down at Asyut, that's the biggest town in Upper Egypt.'

'Asyut, then. We'll hire a launch there,

and meet Kalif coming up. Can you come up behind him?'

'No problem. I'll get a car — there's a road follows the Nile bank. You'll want Elmaza airport.'

'Right, let's move.'

★ ★ ★

'Sure,' Ben Cowan said heartily. 'I appreciate your help.'

He stood at the enquiry desk at Elmaza airport, notepad and ballpoint in hand. He'd made the round of Cairo's hotels; now he was checking flights to Luxor.

He beamed at the clerk behind the desk. 'The good ladies of Boston and Chicago will surely want to see your ancient temples. Many thanks.'

He turned from the counter, putting away his pad. Around him, the busy airport; passengers watching the clock, a policeman patrolling, the noise of engines. Then he saw Shield and Melody crossing towards the booking hall, a porter following with baggage.

Deftly he brought a large handkerchief

from his pocket and mopped his face, casually moving behind a pillar. Shield's voice came clearly. 'Asyut . . . yes, two seats for Asyut please.'

He watched them go through to flight departures and made his way to the restaurant, found a seat where he could watch them over a cup of coffee.

He brought out his pad and checked their departure time; not long to wait. His head turned as he surveyed the hall; no one else appeared to be interested. He sat stirring his coffee and glancing at the *Gazette*; a stout and balding man with time on his hands.

Their flight was called. He watched Shield and Melody go up the steps and into their aircraft. Engines thrummed. The plane taxied, lifted and headed south down the Nile Valley.

Cowan sat and thought about Asyut. He felt rather pleased with himself; time and energy had not been wasted. Obviously they had a lead. He considered his next move.

13

Snatch

Mikhail Sekov, Colonel in the G.R.U.
— army intelligence — sat on a wooden
high-backed chair in a modern flat
overlooking the Nile. One hand gripped
an untasted glass of vodka. He stared
unseeing at cars crossing a concrete
bridge, yachts from the sailing club on
Gezira Island; and, far distant, the small
triangles that were pyramids jutting up
from the desert, blurred in the heat haze.
And sand, sand everywhere, even on the
ledge of the window.

He gulped a mouthful of vodka and his
gaze moved down to palm trees on the
embankment. Palms reminded him of
home, a villa beside the Black Sea, his
wife and family. He turned to look at a
photograph on the plain table beside a
narrow bed, and smiled.

It was a plain room with a single

picture; a reproduction of *Sunflowers* by Van Gogh. Even if Vincent was a painter of the decadent West, the picture reminded him of fields in his own Caucasus, fields stretching to every horizon and filled with ripe yellow flowers. He savoured a memory of mountains at his back, a small port with oil tankers, sunbathers on a beach.

No hope of seeing that for a while . . . he sighed and swallowed more vodka . . . stuck here.

As his thoughts turned to serious matters, his long face took on a lean and wolfish aspect under tufts of grey hair. His eyes turned a blank grey.

The political situation in Egypt had deteriorated in a way that made his superiors unhappy. He, too, was unhappy about the difficulty of operating as more and more Russians returned home; here, he stuck out like a Borzoi at a cat show. And the Praesidium was insisting on regaining a strong influence here in Cairo.

But would Kalif's plot lead to that influence? Privately, Sekov doubted it. He distrusted Kalif — and scowled as he considered Fabian, weak with a loose tongue when he'd been drinking. Which was too often.

The perfume now . . . his mouth set hard as he thought about that. The demonstration had been impressive — if it hadn't been faked. Well, he'd soon know the truth about that. And if it truly worked the way it seemed, he wanted the perfume; that, alone, made it worth going along with.

Fingers drummed on the door — two, one, three.

Sekov rose and crossed the room, unlocked the door. Krim slid inside and Sekov closed and locked the door again. It irked him that Krim should so obviously look the Security man; square shoulders, close-cropped hair, blue serge suit. But always reliable, Sekov reminded himself; and he needed a man he could rely on.

He poured vodka.

'Thank you, Colonel.'

'Everything fixed?'

'Arranged as you ordered Colonel.'

'Good.'

Sekov drained the last of his vodka and looked round the room; it might be the last time he'd see it. If anything went wrong, he was in an impossible position. He glanced at his watch.

'Let's get on with it.'

★　★　★

The plane from Elmaza airport, en route for Luxor, touched down briefly on a strip of flat ground outside Asyut, airscrews stirring up a sandstorm. Shield and Melody descended, hefted bags and walked towards a distant cab-rank. The sun seared like a hot iron, the air stifled and there was no shade at all.

A dark-skinned youth grinned at them as he opened the door of his cab. 'Hotel, yes?'

'Yes. An English-speaking hotel please.'

'Right way, sah. Me first-class driver, very fast. Guide too, and interpreter.'

They got in; and, although the cab had been parked in the shade, the inside was like an oven. Their driver engaged gears and shot away, showering sand and bumping over rock to reach a made-up road.

Asyut grew into a fair-sized town as they approached, new factories sprawling from its edges. Beyond the broad reach of the Nile, white domes dazzled. They swept past rows of neat houses that looked all alike, shops and cafés, and pulled up before a new-looking hotel on the waterfront.

A uniformed porter came out to carry the bags inside and Shield registered at the desk. As they went to their rooms, he said: 'See you on the veranda after a shower.'

Twenty minutes later, they met on the veranda of the hotel, Melody wearing Jeans and T-shirt, Shield comfortable in lightweight slacks and a cotton shirt open at the neck. They sat in wicker chairs at a table under a sunshade with a view of the quayside and limestone blocks being hoisted aboard ships. It was a busy scene with plenty of river traffic.

They sipped ice-cold beer and ate salad. Afterwards, as the heat lessened, they strolled along the riverbank towards a boathouse, where Melody cast a professional eye over a collection of motor launches.

'That one,' she said, pointing to a small cabin cruiser with the name *Ramses II*.

She went shopping while Shield haggled over a price.

'I want to hire her for a trip upriver,' he said. 'About a week of sight-seeing. How much?' He pulled out his wallet and thumbed banknotes.

The boatman rattled off Arabic, mingling it with broken English. 'For hire, yes. One week, good.' He named an excessive price.

After haggling, they agreed on half the original figure, paid over the money and brought their cases from the hotel. When Melody returned with provisions, he said quietly:

'I'd like to leave as soon as we can. We'll be less conspicuous on the river and I don't intend to miss *Isis*.'

Melody nodded and took a look at the engine, checked the fuel tank and bilge. 'Looks okay, Dan. Cast off.'

She started the engine and took the wheel, steering out into mid-stream and turning leisurely to head back towards Cairo. The town vanished behind them, the river stretched ahead, wide and bordered by black mud and green fields that shaded into the yellow of the desert.

Engine throbbing, *Ramses II* coasted along past houses where *fellahin* laboured in fields of cotton and sugar cane and dogs ran barking along the bank. Palms shaded the riverbank and Melody kept close in. They saw water buffalo drinking and a heron fishing. It was quiet and peaceful.

There was no sign of *Isis*.

The sun set in a blaze of purple and gold and Shield moored for the night in a deserted stretch of river. The temperature dropped sharply and they put on sweaters, sitting on deck under the stars.

Shield lit a cigarette. 'Two hour spells,' he said. 'I'll take the first watch. Kalif might travel by night and I don't want him to slip past. There's a chance he won't be expecting opposition from this direction.'

'And then?'

He shrugged. 'Keep an eye on him,

170

play it as it comes.'

Ramses II moved gently at the end of her mooring line. The broad green leaves of the palms turned black. A few stars pierced the night sky above the Nile.

★   ★   ★

The black saloon with tinted windows moved at a sedate speed, drawing no attention to itself. The main road leading south from Cairo was quiet. It was just after two in the afternoon and siesta time; there was little traffic.

Sekov sat in the back of the car, wearing a wide-brimmed hat, gaze fixed on the back of Krim's solid neck. Neither man spoke; all the moves had been decided — all that remained was to put the plan into operation.

The saloon swished past wadis and canals and finally reached the suburb of Maadi. A network of small villas, each set behind a wall, each with its own gate.

Krim slowed and stopped outside one of the villas. He stayed at the wheel and kept the engine running.

Sekov got out, leaving the rear door open. He pulled down the wide brim of his hat and kept his head down, his face in shadow. There was no one in the street. He moved to the gate in the wall and rang the bell.

The sun was hot and he waited patiently. It was the siesta and no one hurried. Slow, dragging feet sounded behind the wall. The gate opened on a chain and a lean brown face showed.

Sekov's fingers, rigid, jabbed into the man's throat. He dropped. Sekov reached a hand through the gap and unhooked the chain, stepped inside and closed the gate; he didn't bother to replace the chain.

The garden had a small ornamental pool and flowing shrubs that partially hid him from the house. He bent over the servant and chopped once, deliberately, with a stiffened hand against the neck; he wanted no live witnesses afterwards.

He moved up to the house. The door stood half-open and it was shadowed and silent inside. He stepped into the hall, listening, took a small glass globe from his pocket and tossed it along the passage.

There was a tinkle of breaking glass and dense smoke billowed up.

Sekov called in Arabic: 'Fire . . . fire!'

Urgent sound of movement came from a room along the passage. Sekov pushed through the smoke as a door opened and a second man showed himself. A karate blow to the neck and this man went down, his head at an unlikely angle.

Sekov stepped into the room. Arabic furnishings. One man. He recognized from photographs the brown face of the prophet of Deir.

The old man rose stiffly from a couch, his face calm. 'Who are you? What is it — ?'

Sekov reached him in three swift paces and felled him with a single blow. The punch was pulled. This man he wanted alive.

The old Bedouin was skin and bone, a lightweight. Sekov hoisted him over his shoulder in a fireman's lift and went back through the smoke-filled passage to the garden. He reached the gate as a curious neighbour showed.

'Phone the fire brigade,' Sekov said briskly. 'The old man has smoke in his lungs — I'm taking him to hospital.'

He eased his burden into the back of the car and climbed in. Krim took off smoothly, turning to head back to Cairo, building up speed.

Sekov looked back but there was no excitement behind him. He took a hypodermic from a case and checked the pulse; steady. Nothing to worry about there, he was a tough old buzzard. He bared Azad's arm and injected him; he'd sleep for twelve hours now.

The kilometres swished by. Krim watched the rear mirror. No pursuit.

They reached Old Cairo and Krim slowed and took a twisting route to reach a yard filled with vehicles. Quickly they transferred the sleeping prophet to a small van, the rear enclosed. Sekov got in the back with Azad.

Krim drove out of the yard and out through backstreets to the embankment. A left turn and dead ahead the bridge to the island of Roda. Both Krim and Sekov tensed; if the news had got ahead of them, this was where a roadblock would be. Nothing.

They crossed the bridge and traversed the island.

The second bridge, to the west bank of the Nile. Again nothing.

Sekov relaxed. Krim turned left into the suburb of Giza, picking up speed, driving past residential houses and office blocks and colleges. At the Technical Institute he took a side road that brought the van to a small jetty.

The hovercraft stood poised on a sloping ramp, bright orange with lettering in both Russian and Arabic:

OIL SURVEY UNIT

Sekov looked round carefully to make sure he was not observed, then carried Azad aboard. Krim drove away to ditch the van elsewhere.

In the cabin of the hovercraft, Sekov laid the sleeping prophet on a bunk and covered him with a sheet. He poured himself a large vodka, satisfied; a tricky operation had gone off well.

14

Confrontation

Ramses II motored north at cruising speed under a clear cobalt sky. She was not new, her paintwork faded and scratched; the small cabin was part of the bow and there was a cramped dark area behind the cabin. Shield stood at the wheel, looking forward over the curved roof of the cabin. Melody was inside, brewing coffee and cutting sandwiches.

There had been no sign of *Isis* during the night and he worried in case Kalif did not intend coming so far upriver.

Melody ducked out through the low cabin door, balancing a jug in one hand and a plate in the other.

They ate breakfast, spelling each other at the wheel.

Shield commented, 'Whoever said dawn was the best part of the day must have been born around here.'

'It beats boating on the Thames,' Melody agreed.

The sun had cleared the horizon in the east but the air was still cold. The muddy river flowed swiftly, sweeping them along between papyrus and palms, passing villages and ancient rock tombs. A *felucca* moved in the opposite direction. Colourful dragonflies hovered.

Beyond green fields cliffs rose on the horizon, marking the beginning of the desert; and now Shield could appreciate how constricted this country was — a few scant miles either side of a river, a fertile valley between bare rock and desert.

He watched fascinated as a peasant worked his *shaduf* — a seesaw with a basket at one end, transferring water from the Nile to an irrigation canal.

A string of barges passed, loaded down with grain. The sun started to burn, the air wavered.

As Shield rigged an awning to protect them from the sun, Melody murmured, 'Kalif!'

He heard the deep throbbing of powerful engines. 'Get down.'

Melody disappeared into the cabin and Shield pretended to struggle with the awning, using it to screen himself as the white yacht slid majestically past. The bow-wave creamed. *Ramses II* bobbed in its wake.

He glimpsed Kalif on deck, sprawled in a canvas chair, his massive hump bared.

Isis rounded a bend and vanished from view.

Shield felt content; contact made. 'Okay now,' he called and Melody came back on deck.

He finished rigging the awning and waited for a steamer to pass, turned in a half-circle. He kept well back, with the steamer between him and Kalif, and followed. He had no intention of losing him now.

'If *Isis* ties up tonight, I'll take a close look at her.'

Melody glanced at him. 'Safia?'

Shield nodded. Remembering Ann Thomas, he worried for her.

The two boats continued south.

★   ★   ★

Al Hakim's office at police headquarters in Cairo was not a large one; a desk with in-and-out trays, two chairs, a filing cabinet. Smoke swirled under the harsh glare of electric light. The captain's head ached.

He threw wide the window and breathed deeply of the cool as dawn broke over the city. It had been a long night, the phone ringing endlessly; detailed reports from Maadi, reports from search parties, pressure from his superiors, newspaper reporters asking questions for which he had no answers.

He tossed a half-smoked cigarette through the window, loosened his tie and rubbed the back of his neck. It would be nice to go home and take a shower, sleep. But that was impossible. His mouth tasted sour and he swallowed water, spat. He crossed to the door, earrings jangling.

'Coffee, Achmed!'

Up all night for what? He stared gloomily at the first reports, his own jottings on a pad by the telephone . . . it rang again. He scooped up the receiver, listened, snarled, 'No, nothing new,' and slammed it back on its cradle.

Worry, that was all he had, worry. He had to bring Azad back alive. A kidnapping had not been anticipated and that — of course — was what had happened. The men he had detailed to protect the prophet had arrived too late; he'd carry the blame for that. He sweated. To survive in office he had to find Azad, and quickly.

He hadn't wanted the nursemaid job, hadn't taken it seriously — but now a crime had been committed his confidence returned. Kidnapping and murder was something he knew how to deal with.

Two men murdered. A professional job. Someone had hired a professional. Who? And why?

To rescue Azad, he first had to locate him; and he had no lead so far. But who would want to kidnap the Prophet? Azad was a Holy One, much respected . . . something to do with this new religion? He'd been onto the local police at Kenel and they'd promised to hunt leads at their end.

Achmed came in with coffee and got

out again quick. His staff didn't want to be around while he was in a savage rage. Almost he smiled, drained the coffee and went to the window.

Al Hakim stared out across a labyrinth of streets, minarets rising tall and golden in the early morning light. No fires burst that he could see and that, at least, was good.

It had been a close-run thing yesterday. When news of Azad spread, the city seethed in foment . . . the hands of unbelievers laid on Allah's Prophet! There had been demonstrations, strikes, windows smashed and cars overturned in the streets, foreigners harassed. The mood of the Cairones had been ugly and only a strong show of force by the police had contained an explosive situation. There would be a few aching skulls this morning — he hoped with more sense in them.

But still the only way to defuse the situation was to get Azad back unharmed. Everything hinged on that.

The routine was in hand; spies everywhere listening and seeking, asking questions. He was the spider at the heart of his web and Al Hakim was an old hand at spinning a web. Now it became a question of time.

All he could do was wait for the break to come. Then he would move, men and machines, very fast indeed. His forces waited. But waiting was the hardest job of all.

He worried in case he did not get word in time.

★ ★ ★

Night pressed a dark bowl over the river. A few stars glittered, shedding pale light. Shield padded along the riverbank, hearing the sound of water through the rushes and the whirr of insects. He moved with stealth from one tree to the next, pausing at each.

An hour had passed since he'd left *Ramses II* and Melody. They had followed *Isis* through the day till she tied up, then dropped back out of sight.

He moved again till, ahead, he glimpsed the shadow-shape of the yacht and approached her the way a cat approaches a sitting bird. One man on deck; only one? No cabin lights. How many crew? Was Safia aboard?

He touched a mooring line and waited, scanning cabin windows, the bridge, the open deck. He was sure now that only one man held the duty-watch.

He went aboard cat-footed and came up behind the sailor as he leaned on a deck rail. One blow to the nape of the neck; carefully he lowered the unconscious man and made a quick tour of the deck. Nobody.

He paused, wary. Would Kalif leave the ship as unprotected as this? The stairway leading down to the cabins stood open, its darkness inviting exploration. Shield went down one step at a time, testing each tread before putting his weight on it. The air was still and warm below. Nothing stirred. He brought a pen-torch from his pocket and flashed it into the cabin — and held his breath.

On a folding table to one side of the cabin he saw a glass vial in the shape of a swan, a vial holding a violet-coloured liquid. Too easy, he thought, smelling bait in a trap. And yet . . .

He had to be sure. He crossed the cabin and lifted the vial in his hand.

At his back, laughter boomed and echoed. Light flooded the cabin, blinding him. Eyes half-shut, he whirled about, pulling the Luger from his belt.

At the top of the stairs stood Suliman Kalif, his great bulk entirely filling the doorway. Smiling, obviously unworried by the gun in Shield's hand, Kalif came slowly and deliberately down the steps and into the cabin. Behind him, on deck, there was the sound of a scuffle.

They faced each other, Shield holding the vial in one hand and a Luger in the other. He was a big man, bigger than most, yet Kalif dwarfed him. The Egyptian was huge and built like a bear with the lump on his back giving him a sinister appearance.

'Stalemate, I think,' Shield said.

Eyes black and hard as slate stared at him. 'You won't shoot,' Kalif said confidently. 'Just look at the top of the stairs.'

A trick? Shield kept his gun steady on

184

the figure in denim battledress as he risked a brief glance at the stairs — and froze. Melody. A dark hand was clapped over her mouth from behind and the blade of a knife was pressed against her throat, making a thin red weal.

'Two can play at night games,' Kalif said.

Shield slowly lowered his gun, bitter and blaming himself. He'd been so sure they hadn't been spotted following the yacht. Obviously Kalif's thugs had sneaked back to grab Melody while he'd been making a careful approach.

'I'll take the gun now.' Kalif held out a big hand. 'You can keep the vial — it's only coloured water.'

Still Shield hesitated.

'Now,' Kalif repeated.

He had no choice; he lowered the Luger and offered it butt-first.

Kalif took the gun. 'Excellent. Now sit down — there.' He pointed to a padded seat along one wall of the cabin.

Shield placed the vial on the table and sat down. Kalif took a seat opposite, lit a cigar and pointed the gun at him.

'Bring the girl here.'

Melody was pushed down the stairs, her hands tied behind her. 'Sorry about this, Dan — I could kick myself.'

Shield nodded, keeping his gaze on the Egyptian. Forcing himself to accept the situation, he controlled his feelings and waited, seeking to find an advantage. 'Any damage?'

'No.' Melody took a seat away from both Shield and Kalif. A dark-skinned sailor with a knife stood beside her. She looked at her most vulnerable and Shield knew it was an act put on to fool the opposition.

'This is the position. If you give trouble, Mr. Shield, the girl dies. If she does, you do.' The voice had the quality of flint. 'Now, there were three of you on the plane from London. Where is the other man?'

He didn't answer at once. Barney must be somewhere on the road behind *Isis*, but how far behind . . . ?

The knife prodded Melody, drawing blood.

'We left Barney in Cairo,' Shield said hurriedly.

Kalif drew on his cigar. 'Why isn't he with you? What is he doing there?'

'Looking for the Russian you had keeping tabs on us.'

'So . . . ' Kalif sat very still. 'You were with Hakim — explain this.'

'Barney knows Hakim — he's been in Cairo before. Anyway, Hakim's been taken off the killing in the perfume bazaar to act as bodyguard to a visiting prophet.'

'Prophet?' Kalif stared at him, then burst into wild laughter. 'Hakim watches the Prophet and your friend seeks the Russian!' The laughter appeared genuine and Shield wondered what the joke was. 'Neither of them will worry us, I think.'

Shield hid relief at taking the heat away from Barney; there was a chance now.

Suliman Kalif finished his cigar. 'That leaves you two. You're persistent, Mr. Shield . . . too persistent for your own good. I don't believe I can allow you to harass us any longer.'

15

Sea of Fire

He came up out of darkness with a furred mouth and a muzzy head. His body jolted with a succession of small shocks; the bare boards in which he lay vibrated. The air carried a sour stale smell.

Shield didn't know exactly where he was except that he was no longer aboard *Isis*. His body felt numb and, when he tried to move, he discovered that his arms and legs were tightly bound with thin cord.

Melody? He rolled sideways and touched a softly-rounded body, bent his head to smell a familiar perfume. The perfume reminded him of Kalif and he shook his head to clear it.

His fingers groped at her; she, too, was securely tied.

And she hadn't come round yet — then he remembered the injection and Kalif's dark face fading out as it took effect.

He waited for his eyesight to adjust to the gloom and made out the shape of an awning overhead. A patch of different dark with stars in it, the silhouette of two men.

He was a prisoner in the back of a truck going somewhere in the night. With an effort, he swayed to his knees, peering forward and out. Two sailors from the *Isis*, both Arab, both armed. They seemed to be driving across empty desert; he saw only sand dunes.

He fell back behind Melody, and began to work on her knots; they were professionally tied and the job was going to take time. How much time did he have?

He worked slowly, fumbling with the smooth cord. Nylon; he'd never break it. A fingernail snagged but he persisted. They had to get free and grab the truck or . . . deep inside, he had a cold feeling that he knew what their fate would be if he failed. He worked steadily but had only loosened one knot when the truck slowed and stopped.

The two Arabs climbed down from the

cab and came round to the back to let down the tailboard. A gun pointed inside. The second man pulled at Shield, rolling him out to sprawl in soft sand. Melody landed on top of him and rolled off; the jolt brought her round.

The Arabs lit cigarettes and walked up and down to stretch their legs. One relived himself against a rear wheel of the truck. Shield's heart sank as he noted how fast the patch of wetness disappeared into the sand.

One of the sailors looked at them and said something in Arabic. The other laughed. Then they both climbed back inside the cab. The engine revved noisily and the truck jerked forward, turned through an arc and drove away. Very soon the sound of its engine faded completely.

Shield blocked out a moment of fear. 'Melody?' His voice held a note of urgency. 'We've got to get free and start moving.'

'All right, Dan.' She still sounded muzzy.

He worked on her knots without speaking. He had an idea what it was going to be like in the desert without water; they wouldn't last long.

It was a slow frustrating business but, finally, he began to make progress. And, as he freed one of her hands, the sun edged above the horizon.

★　★　★

Barney Ryker, at the wheel of a jeep, cursed the dust and the flies as he drove south along the main road from Cairo to Luxor. He had dispensed with his disguise and wore blue-grey slacks and a silk shirt with a neckerchief. His white hair was matted with grey dust.

He drove beside green fields and date palms, with the railway line between him and the Nile. He glimpsed white sails on the river but, so far, had not sighted the *Isis*; he didn't really expect to, not yet. He'd taken his time checking over the jeep, making sure he had the right tools and spares, beer and food before he set out. The first night he'd only got as far as Beni Souef, one hundred and twenty kilometers from Cairo.

He drove carefully at all times but

especially so now; dogs and children and goats had a habit of invading the road at each village he went through. He became interested in improvements that had been made since his last visit; modern houses, water pipes, a combine harvester.

He was further impressed when he saw an orange hovercraft on the river, traveling south at speed. Technology had arrived with a bang. The hovercraft passed him and disappeared from view, and he thought no more of it.

The heat began to get him as he pulled off the road and parked in the shade, had a beer with sandwiches and smoked a cheroot.

He drove on again, watching the river.

Time passed.

Then he noticed a small cabin cruiser moored under trees and thought; that little beaut is just the sort of job Melody would have picked. He stopped and left the jeep, walked across a field to the riverbank. He read the name on her bow: *Ramses II*.

'Dan?' he called.

There was no answer and no one about

so he went aboard and looked in the cabin. He recognized various small items and had little doubt this was the boat Dan and Melody had hired. So where were they?

Frowning. He went back on deck and scrambled on top of the cabin. He had a great view of the river and surrounding land. There was nobody in sight, no hint of movement anywhere. He began to feel uneasy.

He dropped to the deck and made a careful search and new alarm bells started to ring. There were small — but clear — signs of a struggle. His eyes grew bleak as he considered possibilities. It looked as though they'd caught up with Kalif . . . so where was *Isis*?

He went quickly to his jeep and drove on, big hands gripping the wheel, foot hard down. He used all his considerable skill and experiences as a racing driver to make fast time to Asyut and stopped at the boatyard.

The boatman echoed his question. '*Ramses II*, sah? Very good boat, sah, now on hire to English peoples.' Ryker got a description from him and his last doubt vanished.

'A white motor yacht? Yes sah, that passed here some hours ago. Travelling south.'

'Thanks.' Ryker tipped the Arab and went back to his jeep. He pushed on in pursuit of *Isis*.

★ ★ ★

By the time both Shield and Melody stood up, free of their bonds, the sun had climbed above the horizon. A red glow bathed the empty landscape hinting at the heat to come. Shield guessed they had perhaps an hour before they began to roast.

'Which way?' Melody asked in a practical tone. 'Follow the tracks left by that truck?'

'No.' Shield was busy flexing arms and legs to get his blood flowing again. 'They wouldn't make it that easy — probably drove the long way round. Anyway, the wind will cover tracks quickly. We've got to walk in a straight line to the Nile, that's our only chance.'

He studied the vast and desolate landscape around them. Nothing but dunes to every horizon.

'The river runs north-south. Depending on which side we are, we head either due east or due west. How's your memory?'

Melody quoted from a guidebook she'd read on the flight out: 'The Eastern desert. The ground seems to be littered with coloured stones — flint and quartz and black rock. It is a mountainous area. The Libyan desert, to the west of the Nile, is difficult to cross, a desert of dunes — '

'That confirms my own idea,' Shield said. 'There'd be army patrols out on the eastern bank. So we're west of the river and strike due east. We move now and find what shelter we can from the sun, then lay up till dusk. Travel all night.'

They began walking towards the rising sun. The ocean of sand appeared limitless, each dune they passed exactly like the last. A harsh and inhospitable land, silent and arid. They plodded on, sinking ankle-deep in fine dust. As the sun climbed higher, the heat increased. Soon they started to sweat.

Shield had the larger stride and forged ahead. He paused and waited for Melody to catch up. 'We must keep going,' he urged.

'I'm going to freckle like mad,' she said crossly.

Shield smiled and went on, squinting into a haze that was already forming. He lifted his hands and cupped them round his eyes to block out the glare. 'I'm sure that's a rock or something sticking up over there — come on.'

They turned aside and marched on, weary now, clothes glued to their bodies, mouths drying out. A wind came up, a hot dry wind that stirred the surface, burying the tracks they left behind.

Neither mentioned water.

Shield said: 'It is a rock — just keep going a bit longer.'

Eventually, skin burning, they reached the bare crag jutting from the sand and slumped down in its shade.

After a time, he said: 'Try to sleep now.

We'll stay here till dark and then walk east again. Sometime we'll hit the river.'

He didn't say that he doubted if they'd last that long . . .

Melody nodded briefly and closed her eyes, relaxing. 'It's a fraction cooler here.'

But the heat of the day had not arrived. The sun climbed slowly and steadily towards its zenith. Hot air seared their lungs with every breath. Even in the shade the heat was almost unbearable, the rock that sheltered them burned.

Shield tore the buttons off his shirt and handed one to Melody. 'Suck this,' he said. 'It'll help.'

She put it in her mouth without answering.

Their small patch of shade was a life-saver; but it contracted in size as the sun moved directly overhead and they huddled up, panting. Shield had a vision of iced beer — and put the thought from him. Time dragged.

They lay in a stupor, neither waking nor sleeping, as the pitiless heat beat down like waves from a blast furnace. Their parched bodies wilted.

The sun, a blazing disc, traveled through the sky, traveled so slowly that it seemed never to move but always remain suspended above their heads.

The vast sea of sand became an ocean of fire.

The sun lowered itself through the sky, touched the horizon and slowly sank from view. A brief twilight hovered, tinting the sky with green, casting mauve shadows.

Shield made the effort to get to his feet. 'Come on,' he croaked. 'Got to get on. Make as much distance as we can before sunrise.'

Stars glittered dully in a violent night. He took his bearings and moved into the east, one plodding foot after the other. Their shoes sank into the fine sand, slowing them, wasting their scant energy. The dunes became a major obstacle.

The moon came up and the air cooled. Thirst was an agony.

'How far d'you reckon, Dan?'

'Just keep moving — we'll get there.'

There was no sign of life in that barren waste; just dust and sand hills, forever and forever.

Shield walked behind Melody to make sure she kept moving. They were like two zombies, he thought, weak from dehydration: Memory stirred as the cold bit and he pulled off his shirt.

'Catch hold, Melody.' It took an effort to force the words from dried-out lips. 'Keep it flat.'

They walked on, slowly, wearily, across the brown and empty land — side by side, with the shirt stretched flat between them. It served to keep them together as they stumbled on. The desert by moonlight had the appearance of a ghostland; no blade of glass, no tree, no water . . .

Shield pulled himself up sharply. Don't think of water, he told himself.

He shivered in the cold night. His legs trembled. On and on they trudged and the hours passed until sunlight once more gleamed above the horizon.

Shield stopped and felt the shirt with his fingers; it was damp with dew. He moistened Melody's lips, then his own.

'Thanks, Dan,' she said faintly. 'I could do with a drink.'

'Cup your hands.'

As she obeyed, he twisted the shirt tightly, wringing every last drop of moisture from it. She swallowed, then offered her cupped hands. Shield licked them dry.

He put on his shirt again and stared round. Sand hills. No rock for shelter. Nothing.

He pushed Melody into motion and followed behind her, heading towards the rising sun. They kept on but their pace was no more than a crawl now; and still no shelter showed.

The heat started. He pulled his shirt up over his head, just leaving only a small gap to see through.

'Cover your head, Melody.'

They pressed on, seeking shade. The heat sapped their strength and there was only sand and dust and the eternal dunes. The air was an oven, the heat a blanket; every breath scorched their lungs.

They staggered, weaving erratically, under a glaring sun in a bleached sky. The silence eroded their senses.

'Hell,' Melody murmured, though whether she was swearing or commenting on their situation he couldn't tell.

Once, Shield raised his head and saw black dots turning in slow circles, hovering on air currents. Vultures gathered.

The wind rose, lifted dust from the arid surface. A hot wind, the *khamsin*. A dark brown mass like a sand dune moved towards them, its top edge blotting out the sun.

Melody stumbled and fell. Shield dropped beside her and clawed with his hands, scooping a shallow pit. They sprawled side by side in the hollow as a wall of sand swept over them.

Shield pulled Melody's shirts over her face. 'Breathe through it.'

He pulled his own shirt over mouth and nostrils to act as a filter. Dust trickled down his neck, filling the depression. A weight of sand built up. He could see nothing now, only hear the hiss of sand particles as the storm raged.

Hope died. It was up to Barney to get Kalif now . . .

Melody was already unconscious when he passed out.

16

Target Area

Suliman Kalif sat alone in the back of a hired car that bumped over a desert track. He was too big for the car and sprawled diagonally across the back seats. In a way, it was a pity the temple was so isolated; in another, its very isolation was what made the plan possible.

The temple was a small one and not in good condition, away from the usual tourist route and so rarely visited. Kalif had bribed an official in the Department of Antiquities and felt confident that there would be no investigation until it was too late to matter.

He was feeling pleased with life. No one had taken more than casual interest when *Isis* moored at Keneh. Shield and the girl had been disposed of. He had the perfume in his pocket. And, shortly, Sekov would arrive with Azad.

The driver — one of his own crew — took the car through the village of Deir, a huddle of mud huts built around an oasis; there was a deep pool and a cluster of date palms. The villagers provided not only a work force, but the first worshippers of the new religion that provided them with a better living than they could remember.

He thought of Safia, frowning. She had proved awkward after the drug had worn off; she hadn't wanted to go into the desert with Fabian. And a lot depended on her performance.

The driver reached a turn-off and sent the car jolting over sand and loose rock towards a small hill. On the hill stood the temple. It looked more impressive now the sand drift had been cleared away and Fabian had done some reconstruction on it.

The temple at Deir was built of limestone and oblong in shape with a flat roof. The outside walls were in poor repair except for the pillars of the ceremonial gateway. The car drove in through the gate and stopped in an open court.

Kalif left the car, walked across the courtyard and into a hall with a flat roof supported by massive stone columns. A statue of Isis dominated the hall. The walls were lined with a frieze of carved reliefs that glowed with brilliant colour now that Fabian had repainted them. It was easy to imagine how this place had appeared in ancient times to superstitious peasants; it would serve again.

Fabian's voice held a note of sharpness. 'No, not like that! You're a queen and I want you to act like one. Let's try that again.'

Safia was dressed as Cleopatra in soft linen of royal purple, the double crown on her head. She saw Kalif and turned away.

'Suliman, I'm tired of this. And I don't want to have to wear that perfume again.'

'It is necessary,' he said flatly.

We'll have to put her under right away, he thought, and keep her under. And wondered if there'd be long-term effects.

He stared round the hall, at the friezes and torch-holders, the serpent goddess of Lower Egypt and the vulture goddess of Upper Egypt.

'You've done well, Phil. I take it you're about ready?'

Fabian gestured at the girl. 'I'm ready — she isn't.'

Kalif's voice was iron. 'Safia will do as I say. Now show us the underground chamber.'

As they walked to a doorway at the rear of the hall, Fabian asked: 'When's Azad due to arrive?'

'Soon . . . soon, Phil.'

★　★　★

After the *khamsin* blew itself out, Ben Cowan crawled out from his shelter and shook the dust from his clothes. He took a long drink and considered whether or not to go on; not too seriously, because he knew he had little option. But he carefully checked his compass before finally making up his mind.

He adjusted the Arab burnous over shirt and slacks. It was not worn as a disguise, but simply because it was sensible clothing for desert travel. He packed away the opaque sheet of plastic stretched at an angle from the camel's saddle and methodically cleaned his rifle.

Then he climbed into the saddle and nudged the camel. It rose up and he pointed it south.

He was not far inland from the west bank of the Nile and moving parallel to it. After the train journey to Asyut where he learnt that *Isis* had passed through and that Shield had hired a boat, he decided on a camel. He hoped to pass unnoticed away from the more usual routes.

But now he was beginning to have doubts; the storm had shaken him and the motion of the camel gave him a permanent uneasy feeling in his stomach. Maybe he was just getting old.

He rode on across the trackless desert, the dunes rising and falling like the waves of a great ocean. The sun was past its zenith and sinking slowly towards the horizon but it was still hot. He watched his compass bearing continually.

Small specks in the sky attracted his attention. Birds hovering. As he watched, they descended in lazy circles. Vultures. It occurred to him that some other desert traveler was in trouble and he turned his camel in that direction. The birds were down, out of sight behind the dunes and he urged his camel to speed.

He saw wavering tracks in the sand and, beyond the sand hills, two figures sprawled out under the sun. The vultures had landed near them. One of the figures weakly waved an arm to keep the birds away.

Cowan drew his rifle and fired a single shot over their heads. Instantly the birds took flight. He rode on and recognised Shield and the girl; they both appeared to be in a bad way.

When he reached them, he forced the camel to its knees slid from the saddle. He pulled a water bottle from his pack and moistened first the girl's lips, then Shield's. He was relieved to see they both responded.

Holding the bottle tightly, he allowed them both to drink a little before he took it away. 'That's enough, I guess — sure mustn't overdo it at first.'

He erected his plastic shelter to give them protection from the sun, then gave them a little brandy.

Shield propped himself up on one elbow, looking dazed. 'It's Cowan, isn't it?' He turned his head. 'Melody?'

'She's going to be okay. You're both going to be okay — just take it easy.'

Cowan got a portable stove working and heated a can of meat broth. 'Get this down and you'll feel better.'

They sipped the hot soup and felt strength return. Cowan produced a tube of sunburn cream.

As Shield rubbed the cream into Melody's raw skin, he said: 'Lucky for us you happened along. You saved our lives. Thanks.'

'What were you doing out here, on foot?' Cowan asked.

'Following a man called Kalif, till he left us in the middle of nowhere.'

'*Isis* is still heading south, Mr. Shield.'

Melody sat up. 'You seem to know about Kalif, Mr. Cowan — d'you think I might have some more brandy?'

'Sure thing.' He passed the flask. 'Don't overdo it now — it's quite a stop to the nearest bar.'

Shield looked at the rifle. 'I may have heard that before, in the City of the Dead.'

Cowan nodded. 'That was me, Mr. Shield. I had an object in view, thought you might lead me to Kalif. And you took me a step of the way.'

'So you know about the scent?'

'Scent?' Cowan looked puzzled. 'You've lost me there,'

Shield gave a brief account of the perfume that had brought them to Egypt and Cowan remained silent a long time.

'I don't like the sound of this stuff,' he said finally. 'This is news to me, but it adds up to something nasty. Did you hear that Prophet, Azad, had been snatched? There's a pattern to these things.'

'Like the Russian you warned us about?'

'Small beer, but he works for Sekov, and Sekov is the real McCoy. I couldn't figure why Kalif and Sekov got together.'

'What's your interest?' Melody asked.

Cowan ignored the question. 'You're not far from the river — you almost made it.' He brought a plastic jerry-can from the pack on his camel. 'Water. I'll leave this and the shelter. Stay here till sunset then head east to the river. I'm going after Kalif. Fitting the pieces together, I have a notion I'll find him somewhere around Deir.'

Shield said grimly, 'I've an account myself to settle with Kalif.'

'That's fine by me, just so long as you leave my name out of any official accounting you have to do.' He handed Shield his rifle. 'I may need someone at my back this time.'

Ben Cowan mounted his camel and rode away to the south.

★   ★   ★

The bright orange hovercraft came in from the desert, throwing up a spume of sand across the setting sun.

Sekov had left the Nile some thirty kilometres from Keneh and made a wide loop out through the empty dunes. The hovercraft was too conspicuous for him to risk going directly to the temple; there was no point in giving away their location before they were ready.

He felt relaxed now he was out of sight. Going down the Nile had been an ordeal; if anyone had got aboard and found Azad he knew he would have been staked out in the desert. The Prophet had quietened down; at first, when he'd recovered consciousness he had cursed Sekov tirelessly.

He arrived at Deir at dusk, timing it so that he had enough light to see by but not so much that he would be immediately obvious from the distant village. He drove in between tall pillars to the open court and switched off the engine. Slowly the hovercraft sank to the ground. He climbed out, stretching.

Kalif came from the inner hall of the temple. 'Is everything okay? No trouble?'

'No trouble. I've got Azad here.' Sekov reached in and pulled the Arab out of the hovercraft.

Azad stared round him, spat at Kalif. 'This is Deir. Do not think you can pretend to me — I know. This is the old temple and you are the blasphemers who seek to corrupt the word of Allah and bring back false gods.'

Kalif didn't bother with a reply. His big hands closed on the Prophet, propelling him into the covered hall where Fabian was touching up a relief carving.

Sekov followed. The Russian looked round, appraising; it was his first visit to the temple and he was impressed. His gaze travelled round the statues and paintings to the wall niches, in each of which was set a mask of one of the gods of ancient Egypt. The masks looked mysterious and sinister.

'You've done a good job here,' he told Fabian.

Azad stood with disapproval. 'A curse on the enemies of Allah! There is but one God and His vengeance shall be mine. The anointed will rise as one and destroy this abomination!'

Fabian stared at the old bedouin and shook his head in admiration. 'A wonderful old boy. They'll follow him right enough.'

Kalif turned to face Sekov. 'I've had the girl put under — she was beginning to get out of hand. I intend to keep her drugged now. We'll put Azad in with her.'

Sekov stiffened. So Kalif had turned on the girl already . . . he wondered who would be next.

'Is that wise? How will she react after a time?'

'I don't know,' Kalif said bluntly. 'Doctors can take care of it — afterwards.'

He led the way to the back of the hall. A doorway led to a long passage that sloped downward. A number of small chambers branched off from the passage.

'Solid rock,' Kalif said. 'I've had an air-tight door fitted.'

They continued to the end of the passage.

Sekov made a smile. 'Well, we'll soon know how Azad reacts and that's the important thing.'

⋆ ⋆ ⋆

Ryker was dead-beat by the time he reached Keneh, seventy kilometres north of Luxor. He'd been pushing hard through the heat of the day and still hadn't seen *Isis*.

As he slowed to go through the small town, it occurred to him that he couldn't go on much longer without a break. Commonsense told him it wouldn't help Dan or Melody if he had an accident.

He found a hotel, parked and went in to book a room. He showered and changed, ate a meal and rested till late afternoon. Then he went down to the riverfront to ask questions and found they weren't necessary. Almost the first thing he saw was the sleek shape of Kalif's yacht, moored just south of the town.

He strolled along the bank, a tourist casually admiring the river and boats against a setting sun; but his sharp eyes studied *Isis* from a distance. No sign of Kalif. He considered going to the police, but Al Hakim had said Kalif had protection and this was a time far caution till he found Dan and Melody. Information was what he wanted.

Any ship that puts into harbour is of interest to boatmen the world over; they quickly get to know the who and where of any craft. Ryker saw a riverman sitting on his own and joined him.

Neither spoke, though the boatman turned his head once, and then continued his silent study of the water. Ryker took out his wallet and counted off five notes. He tucked them into the man's hand and spoke softly in Arabic.

'I'm interested in the white yacht. Interested in knowing if there's a European with a red-haired girl aboard. And where the owner is.'

A dark hand closed round the notes and they vanished into the folds of a *galabia*. 'Wait here.'

Ryker lit a cheroot and contemplated the effect of sunset on the water, but his heart wasn't in it. He was worried for Dan and Melody, more worried than he cared to admit.

After a while, the riverman returned.

'Only the crew are aboard now. There is no European or red-haired girl. The owner hired a car and one of the crew drove it. They took the road towards Deir.'

Damn funny, Ryker thought; where the hell are they? He'd shared both good times and danger with Dan and Melody

215

and a strong bond had formed between them. His anxiety now was almost a physical thing.

'Thanks, friend.' He rose and tossed the stub of cheroot into the water and returned to the hotel. He unfolded a map and studied it; Deir was a small oasis in the desert, some thirty kilometers from Keneh to the east.

He went out to his jeep und drove out along the road to Deir by moonlight.

⋆ ⋆ ⋆

Al Hakim stalled for time, ignoring the questions of both superiors and news-men. He had put out one routine announcement: 'The police are pursuing their enquiries'.

It would have been difficult to put out anything more. He sat at his desk with a cup of cold coffee, his eyes red-rimmed with fatigue. He'd already quit smoking and started again. He was seriously beginning to think this was one case he wouldn't crack in time.

Spider-like, the police captain sat at the

heart of his web, his patience wearing thin. The web wasn't offering much in the way of flies.

Two Europeans, one speaking Arabic; no satisfactory description of either.

A black saloon car, since found abandoned.

And no lead to where Azad might be. Or who had snatched him. Or why.

He sighed a little as he sat brooding. The phone rang.

'Cairo police. Captain Hakim.'

'Keneh police station, sir. You asked us to report any developments — '

Al Hakim took a quick breath, his brain clearing. 'You've located Azad?'

'No sir, there's no sign of the Prophet. But the man I posted at Deir reports increased activity at the temple. People arriving. Also the atmosphere in the village — he thinks something big is happening there. There's nothing definite, just a feeling of mounting tension.'

Al Hakim's thoughts moved swiftly. The Prophet came from Deir — he vanished — now things are happening there. A hunch formed.

'Keep the temple under observation but don't interfere. I'm coming down to take charge.'

He slammed down the phone and pushed back his chair, knotted a tie and slipped on his jacket. The idea of action braced him. Maybe there was nothing to it — but he had to look as though he were doing something. And this could be the lead he needed.

He stormed through the outer office, shouting: 'Phone the airport I'm on my way. Have the helicopter warmed up. Tell my special squad to stand ready.'

He left almost at a run.

17

The Temple at Deir

Mikhail Sekov moved easily and quietly outside the ruined wall marking the limits of temple ground. The sun was climbing into a morning sky. He paused occasionally to inspect the ancient stonework. Sometimes there was a gap in the wall that allowed him a view through to the temple building inside.

Although he made no effort to hide himself — why should he? — his circuit of the wall was not obvious and he did not think anyone observed him.

Sekov felt dissatisfaction with his role in the Syndicate; his suspicions about Kalif had grown since he'd learnt the Egyptian had used the perfume on Safia and shut her away. Now the hunchback stalled when he suggested it was time to see how Azad was reacting. Kalif pretended he was busy helping Fabian with the priests' robes they were to wear for the ceremony.

So Sekov prowled outside the temple, checking the possibility of a second tunnel leading to the underground chambers.

He followed the uneven wall towards the rear of the temple, paused as he was about to step round a fallen block of stone. He saw a line of footprints in the sand, going away from him. It seemed doubtful that they were made by one of Fabian's helpers from the village; this was an unlikely spot for a workman. The prints were freshly made and led from the dunes; made by boots, not sandals. Someone, he decided, was spying on them.

He drew a Russian automatic from his pocket and advanced cautiously, following the prints, silent as a hunting wolf. Round a corner, he came to a break in the wall. A man in a burnous lay flat on the ground, peering over a fallen slab, directly into the inner hall.

Sekov aimed his gun at the man and spoke softly in Arabic. 'Keep your hands where I can see them and stand up facing me.'

A head turned to look up at him. 'Take it easy, pal. Just curious, is all.' The voice sounded American.

'Get up.'

The watcher rose. 'This temple's listed in the official guide, you know. Nothing secret about it.'

Sekov kept his automatic leveled. 'Go through the gap into the temple.'

'This is ridiculous. I'm only doing a job here. Ben Cowan's my name and I'm with an American agency, checking on facilities for our tours. You can easily — '

'Inside!' Sekov spoke sharply, his finger white on the trigger.

Cowan shrugged and climbed over the stone slab into the courtyard. Sekov followed. 'Keep moving.'

Cowan took his time crossing the court, looking about him with interest. 'Got up real nice, pal.'

The immense figure of Suliman Kalif loomed in the entrance to the inner hall. 'Who is this?' he demanded suspiciously.

'I caught him spying on us.'

Cowan protested indignantly. 'Spying, nothing! I was just admiring the temple and the work you guys have put in here. Great job.'

Kalif stared intently at the prisoner. 'Do you know him, Sekov?'

'No, but I doubt that he's connected with tourism.'

Kalif's big hands gripped Cowan, tore away the burnous, found a passport and flipped through it. 'It doesn't greatly matter who he represents . . . it's too late for anyone to interfere. I'll put him in with Safia and the old man.'

He puhed Cowan towards the rear of the hall. Sekov followed.

★　★　★

The track leading across the desert from Keneh to Deir was scarcely more than a vein of bare rock partially hidden by wind-driven sand and Shield drove with extra care; he had no wish to be lost in the desert a second time.

It had turned out a shorter walk to the river than either he or Melody had anticipated and, by a stroke of luck, they had come on the Nile at Azyut. After a meal, and a bath and some essential shopping. Shield had hired a car and set off, following the river bank to Keneh. A glimpse of the *Isis* moored there had convinced him that Cowan knew what he was talking about.

Melody sat in the back of the car, Cowan's rifle gripped in her hands, eyes watchful. 'Barney should be ahead of us now.'

'So look out for him.'

The sun was high, the sky a bright blue. Heat poured down. The car bumped and jolted over the track as it snaked between lines of ochre dunes. It was a barren, silent land. Time passed until Melody said:

'Trees ahead. Either Deir, or a mirage.'

The air wavered in the heat, but as Shield drew closer he saw the oasis was no mirage. The palms were real. A small village, mainly small houses of dried mud and bricks, had grown up around a deep waterhole in the desert. The only sign of life were the barking dogs; the villagers would be out of the sun, taking their siesta. Near the pool, under the shade of palm-leaves, he saw a jeep with a man sleeping in the back.

He parked beside the jeep as Melody shouted: 'Barney!'

Ryker started up out of sleep, staring at them as if they were ghosts. 'Jesus, you two scared the hell out of me — where've you been?' He reached down between his feet and hauled up three cans of beer. 'This calls for a celebration.'

Melody took the beer. 'Could've done with this twenty-four hours back . . . '

Ryker listened in grim silence as Shield briefly told their story. 'I reckon we might have to take drastic action about Kalif — and I don't think Hakim will object.'

Shield asked, 'Have you seen anything of Cowan?'

'Not a sign.'

'What's the position here?'

'Kalif's at the temple, down a track that way.' Ryker jerked a thumb. 'My guess is most of the village is there too. I was planning on making mine a night visit.'

Shield deliberated. 'Yes, night will be

best, I think — let's get some sleep while we can.'

★   ★   ★

Shield woke with a light breeze stroking his face and felt refreshed. An oasis with a pool and the shade of palms could be a pleasant place, he reflected; the heat of the day had passed and long shadows lay across the dunes.

Melody slept beside him.

Ryker sat alert in the back of the jeep, the rifle in his hands. 'I think we should move, Dan. The local cop was taking an interest in us a while back.'

Shield nodded and started the engine. He left the village and headed out into the desert; the track seemed to go on until the horizon.

Melody woke with a yawn. 'What goes on?'

'Left for the temple,' Ryker directed.

Shield turned. The new track was even fainter and he had to concentrate to follow it by starlight. Presently the silhouette of a building, long and flat, showed on the crest of a hill.

'That's it,' Ryker said.

Shield drove the truck off into the desert, swinging behind a row of high sand dunes. He stepped out of sight of the temple.

'What's the plan?' Melody asked.

'D'you still have your Arab gear, Barney?'

'Yep.'

'You and I will go in close. Melody, I want you to stay outside and cover us. We'll look the place over before we decide anything — if Safia's there, I want to bring her out.'

Ryker rummaged in a suitcase and handed Shield a burnous. 'You take that, Dan.' He slipped on the old *galabia* and wrapped the turban round his head to cover his hair. 'If we're challenged, leave the talking to me.'

The moon came out as they set off on foot for the temple, limestone blocks glistening white in the moonlight.

'Looks romantic,' Melody murmured.

They reached the outer wall and Shield paused, listening to the chatter of voices.

'Seems to be quite a crowd. Stay here, Melody.'

She nodded and crouched behind a fallen slab of stone, cradling the rifle.

Shield and Ryker followed the wall to the open gateway and went in between the truncated stone pillars. The courtyard was filled by men from the village; there was an air of suppressed excitement about the gathering, as if they were waiting for something to happen.

Shield kept to shadow as much as he could, edging round the crowd, making towards the colonnade that marked the entrance to a covered hall. He reached the pillars and waited, studying the temple; it was larger than he had first imagined and there was occasional movement in and out of the hall. He waited till he saw another group enter, then tapped Ryker's arm.

Casually, they tagged on behind the group and moved inside.

The roof was supported by a number of thick stone pillars and they slipped behind one close to the wall. No one seemed to notice them and Shield relaxed, studying his surroundings. No sign of Kalif.

There was a statue of a goddess with fresh offerings at the base; carved reliefs, freshly painted — ancient Egyptians in pink and white and black in traditional posturings; masks of the gods set in niches in the wall. At the back was an open doorway.

He pointed and nudged Ryker.

They moved quietly through the shadows, from pillar to pillar, working their way nearer the door. Nobody went in or out. They waited.

'Chance it,' Shield murmured.

Boldly they walked through the doorways to a long and gloomy passage that sloped down into the ground.

* * *

The army helicopter flew south, following the Nile. In the co-pilot's seat, Al Hakim chewed the end of a cigarette to shreds as he wondered if he were taking the right action. He had to produce Azad alive . . . but suppose he was flying away from where the Prophet was being held?

The cabin behind him held ten uniformed policemen, each carefully hand-picked, each armed with a machine-pistol. His special squad.

The noise of the engine drowned out conversation as the big chopper soared above the river like an outsize dragonfly, its rotor blades carving a silver circle.

He looked down at the river, studying its many bends and the boats moving slowly up and down its length. The fertile green belt sandwiched between desert, all that made life possible, appeared dangerously narrow. He picked out landmarks; the rock tombs at Beni Hazan, Asyut Dam, the temple of Abydes.

His mind went back to Azad. Why had there been no ransom demand? Perhaps the Prophet was already dead — but then why snatch him at all if someone wanted him dead? Al Hakim felt frustrated.

'Keneh,' the pilot shouted above the engine noise, pointing ahead.

Al Hakim jerked a hand downward; he wanted to pick up the local police chief before flying on to Deir. It was essential to have someone with local knowledge.

Keneh looked like a toy town, blood-red in an evening light. The plane dropped steeply and landed on flat ground beyond the town, rotor churning up a dust cloud.

A police car drove slowly towards them and the passenger waited till the dust settled before getting out. As the rotor stopped, he came running and Al Hakim read excitement in his face.

18

The Queen-Goddess

Kalif stood very still. Fabian was a fool, but he still needed him. He controlled his fury and kept his voice steady.

'If you let me down, Phil, you're through. You understand? Sober up long enough to carry off this ceremony and you'll have all the booze you want for the rest of your life.'

The bony archaeologist fumbled with the flapping robes of a High Priest of Isis, his gait unsteady and his speech slurred. The look of low cunning in his eyes fooled nobody. 'Only a li'l drink,' he muttered. 'One li'l whisky to see me through. I'll be all right.'

'See that you are,' Kalif said sharply.

The chamber beneath the temple was lit by a portable electric lamp. Sekov adjusted his own robe, using the movement to keep his face in shadow. His

231

voice held disgust. 'The man's not to be trusted.'

Neither are you, Kalif thought, dark face impassive. He had gone to some trouble to ensure that Fabian was without whisky; but Sekov, he knew, had brought vodka in the hovercraft and it was vodka that Fabian had been drinking . . .

Yes, it was certainly time to take care of Sekov. The Russian had served his purpose. It was obvious he wanted the perfume for his Masters in Moscow . . . a good thing his assistant, Krim, was still in Cairo.

Kalif brought a flat tin from under his pleated linen; he opened it to offer small white plugs. 'Don't forget these, Phil.'

Fabian took two filter plugs with an unsteady hand. 'Be all right,' he said, and wandered away.

Kalif offered the tin to Sekov. 'We'll bring up Safia and Azad now.'

As they fitted the plugs in their nostrils, Sekov said: 'I'll be interested to see the Prophet.'

Kalif smiled thinly. I bet you will, he thought. He picked up the lamp and led the way out of the chamber.

The passage sloped down past a labyrinth of empty chambers cut into solid rock. There was dust underfoot. They moved silently in sandals through gloomy shadows.

Things were still under control. Cowan didn't bother him; whoever had sent him had left it too late. Fabian, he knew from past experience, would get over his drunk. He was more concerned about Safia — he would need her for a time after the ceremony. How long would she last under the effect of the perfume?

They were deep under the surface now, approaching the door at the far end of the passage. Kalif set the lamp down on the floor and brought out a key. He unlocked the door and opened it.

Sekov's wolfish face showed impatience. He brushed past Kalif, pushed the door wide, eager to see Azad for himself. Too eager. His natural caution deserted him.

The room was just a hollow cut out of rock, centuries before, with a small hole high up for ventilation. Lamplight revealed Azad, Safia and Cowan sitting on the floor, backs to the wall. They were motionless, as if frozen, their faces lacking any expression.

Sekov sucked in air. 'So it does work — '

The Kalif's huge hands closed round his throat, choking off sound and breath. The hands tightened until Sekov bent back, face contorted in agony, tightened and twisted till the neck snapped.

★ ★ ★

The passage seemed to descend into an endless dark. Shield advanced warily, feeling his way by a hand on the rough stone, with Ryker close behind. When his eye adjusted to the gloom he became aware that there were openings off the main passage, doorless chambers opening into total darkness. He paused to make a mental note of each; getting lost in a subterranean maze would be no joke.

A light glimmered far off and voices echoed hollowly from rock walls.

He touched Ryker's arm and drew him into one of the chambers. It was dark as a tomb and Ryker flicked on a pen-torch and flashed it around; just an empty room with bare walls and litter on the floor. No one was likely to come here.

Shield pressed back against the wall, listening. The footsteps sounded uncertain. He heard slurred speech, someone muttering to himself. He couldn't make sense of the words. The voice and footsteps faded.

They waited.

More footsteps echoed, the slap-slap of sandals on bare stone; more than one person this time.

Ryker froze in deep shadow as light spilled across the doorway. A voice speaking Arabic:

'Who are you?'

For one wild moment, Ryker thought he had been seen, but a girl's voice answered:

'I am the goddess Isis — ' Her voice held a strangely detached quality — 'Isis wearing the form of the reborn Cleopatra, Queen of all Egypt.'

'Who am I?'

'You are Suliman Kalif, my Grand

Vizier, overseer of all my works in the Two lands.'

Ryker's skin prickled as he listened; what kind of charade was this?

Kalif's voice changed subtly: 'And who are you?'

The voice of an old man, with that same detached quality, replied: 'I am Azad, known as the Prophet of Deir.'

'Which God do you worship?'

'I worship the goddess Isis, now wearing the body of the reborn Queen.'

'What is your duty?'

'My duty is to serve Cleopatra — Isis. My duty is to lead the true believers against those who would oppose her.'

'Good.' Kalif sounded pleased.

Footsteps continued and faded away up the passage.

In the darkness, Ryker whispered: 'Jesus, does he really think he can get away with that stuff?'

Shield said: 'What was it about?' and Ryker gave him a terse exposition.

Shield thought it through as he listened. Obviously, both Safia and Azad had been doped with Cole's perfume;

they were puppets with Kalif pulling the strings. And Kalif was playing for the highest stake . . . the religion of ancient Egypt revived . . . a new Cleopatra to rule the country, with Kalif the power behind the throne. The Prophet had an immense following — but would his supporters switch from Islam to Isis?

He felt grim. 'Whether he can get away with it or not, there's going to be bloodshed. Remember, Azad was preaching a Holy War when he was in Cairo. We've got to stop this.'

Footsteps sounded again and a shadowy figure lurched into the chamber and collided with him.

★　★　★

Melody Gay, in jeans and shirt, lay flat in the sand outside the temple wall, peering over a fallen slab of stone into the open courtyard. The temperature had dropped and she wished she'd brought a sweater with her. She held the rifle off the ground to keep out dust. It seemed a long time since Dan and Barney had slipped through the dark opening at the back of the hall.

The moon cast a pale light over the white limestone temple. What was going to happen here? she wondered. Something was, that was certain. She looked over the crowd of visitors in the courtyard; they had the air of people prepared to go on waiting for a long time. Here and there, a dark face glistened with excitement.

If there was a signal, she missed it. The crowd surged forward as one animal, pouring from the court into the inner hall. Torches were lit in the hall, flaming torches set in wall niches that threw yellow flame and weaving shadows. A relief carving of the serpent-goddess appeared to writhe as the light danced.

Melody felt deserted, alone under the high stars. The babble of voices hushed.

She rose to her feet, taking great care to make no sound and climbed over the stonework. The broken wall gave shadow and she moved swiftly towards the pillars lining the entrance to the great hall.

Silence.

She peered round a stone column; everyone faced away from her. Her gaze darted over the paintings, the statue. From the darkness at the rear stepped an immense figure of a man, hump-backed; there could be no mistaking Suliman Kalif and her eyes widened as she saw he was dressed in the linen of ancient Egypt and bearing the flail of vizier.

He came slowly and solemnly from the door through which Dan and Barney had gone earlier . . . did that mean they'd been caught? She took a firm grip on her rifle.

A smaller figure emerged from the shadow behind Kalif; one she recognised instantly. Safia.

But now the young Egyptian girl looked very different from the dancer at the *Blue Sphinx*. She looked every inch a queen. She wore the royal robe of purple with the double-crown of Egypt on her head. A gold bracelet in the shape of a serpent coiled about one arm and she carried a sceptre. Her face was painted. She moved regally, ignoring the crowd.

Melody watched her eyes, sure that she

was drugged by the perfume.

Kalif the vizier and Cleopatra the queen advanced across the hall. They stopped before the statue of Isis.

The other figures loomed behind them; one a robed priest and the other a weather-beaten Arab in flaming burnous.

19

Last Rites

As the unknown collided with him in the darkness, Shield pinned his arms with one hand and clapped the other over his mouth. He dragged his prisoner further into the chamber below the temple.

'Torch, Barney.'

Ryker played the light from a pen-torch over a gaunt and sunburned face. It was not the face of an Arab. The man was dressed as a priest of ancient Egypt and clutched a vodka bottle in one hand.

Shield said quietly: 'Let out a yell and you'll get hurt. Understand?' He took his hand away from his mouth,

'Careful,' the man slurred. 'It's the only bottle I've got.'

Ryker took the bottle from him as Shield crowded him into a corner.

'What's your name?'

'Philip Fabian.' He had a kind of

drunken dignity. 'Archaeologist.'

'The temple and the dressing up is your idea, is it?'

'Scared me for a moment,' Fabian said. 'Thought you were Sekov — don't trust that bastard.'

Shield recalled that Cowan had mentioned the name.

Fabian said: 'Yes, it's my idea — I need a drink.'

'When you've answered a few questions. Have you seen a stout, bald-headed American here? Cowan?'

'Cowan.' Fabian blinked owlishly. 'Seen him. A spy, Sekov said . . . locked in with the girl and old Azad.'

'Locked in where?' Shield asked patiently.

'Chamber. At the end of this passage.'

'All right. Get his clothes off, Barney and change with him. He'll have some kind of filter plugs somewhere — you'll want those too.'

'Filters.' Fabian swayed against the wall, proudly holding out two white plugs.

'Thanks, mate.' Ryker stripped the archaeologist and put on the robes of an Egyptian priest.

'You can't do it, you know,' Fabian said. 'You don't know the ceremony — Kalif'll be mad.'

Ryker grinned. 'Reckon that's true, cobber.' He handed him the vodka bottle. 'Drink up.'

Fabian grabbed the bottle and sank to the floor with it.

Ryker screwed the plugs into his nostrils as Shield said: 'You'll have to play for time. I'll see if I can find Cowan, and eliminate Sekov. Ad lib till I get back.'

'Okay, Dan.'

Shield borrowed Ryker's torch and went to the doorway. The passage beyond was dark, silent. He moved quickly down the passage. The walls were bare rock with other doorless chambers opening off.

At the far end he saw a door and a crumpled figure on the ground. A man in priest's robes. He stooped and touched the body; neck broken. He had no doubt this was Sekov.

The door was solid, and locked. He searched the body; no key. If Cowan was inside, he'd have to wait. He stripped

Sekov and put on his robes, found a pair of nose filters and inserted them. Then he started up the passage.

Voices. A light gleamed somewhere ahead. Shield ducked into the first empty chamber and waited.

* * *

Ryker stood silent and motionless, blind in the dark chamber. He was aware of Fabian's heavy breathing, the clink of bottle against stone. The archaeologist wasn't going to bother anyone.

Kalif's voice boomed out, echoing along the passage. 'Phil, where are you?' The echoes held notes of impatience. 'Come here — I'm waiting.'

Ryker leant over Fabian and murmured: 'Stay quiet, friend. Concentrate on your drinking.'

He stepped out into the passage and walked up the slope towards the light held in Kalif's hand.

'Are you sober yet?'

'Sober enough,' Ryker answered, faking his voice. Dressed as a High priest of Isis, with Kalif expecting Fabian, there was a chance he could maintain the deception.

Kalif barely glanced at him. 'Come. It's getting late.' He turned and walked ahead, up the passage.

Ryker followed, but not too closely.

At the top of the passage, where it opened into the inner hall of the temple, a young Egyptian girl and an old Arab stood like a pair of statues waiting to be called to life. Ryker's flesh crawled as he looked at them, and he prayed that the filter plugs in his nostrils worked efficiently. He remembered Ann Thomas and did not like the idea of being close to either of them.

Cleopatra wore fine linen of deep purple; the Arab a simple burnous.

'It is time to begin,' Kalif said. 'Follow me. Phil, prompt them as necessary.'

He put down the lamp and moved out into the hall, towards the statue of Isis that dominated the temple. There were offerings in gold dishes at the foot of the statue. He made a commanding figure dressed as a vizier of ancient Egypt.

Cleopatra followed behind him, aloof,

her bearing regal. Ryker and the Prophet walked behind her.

Stone pillars gleamed like ivory by torchlight and shadows moved under the flat roof. Yellow flame lit dark expectant faces in the waiting crowd.

Trumpets sounded a fanfare.

Silence.

Kalif halted in front of the statue and raised his arms, intoning:

'The Queen is dead, the Queen lives forever. Isis returns to claim her own as the reborn Cleopatra, Queen of Queens, ruler of all Egypt. See and acknowledge the Queen-Goddess!'

Safia moved with stately steps towards the statue of the goddess. The gold crown on her head glinted in the light of torches. Her expression was haughty.

Masks of the old gods looked down from niches in the wall. The crowd chanted.

Ryker sweated. If she really needed prompting, he was stuck. Where the hell had Dan got to? He needed a line to follow . . .

He felt a light touch on his arm and

glimpsed the shadowed figure of a priest behind him.

Shield's voice was an urgent whisper: 'Translate for us, Barney.'

The great hall of the temple vibrated to the royal voice of Cleopatra:

'Suliman Kalif presents himself as my Grand Vizier. Know then that he misrepresents himself, that I disown him. He is a common thief and murderer!'

Kalif gave a start and wheeled about, gripping his flail and staring in shock at the painted face of Safia.

Azad, prompted by Ryker, stepped forward. His voice rang through the hall like a great bell.

'You know me, people of Deir. I am your prophet and I, too, speak against Suliman Kalif who would have you worship old gods. False gods! I proclaim Allah to be the one true God and Kalif his enemy and mine!'

Silence followed and lay like a pall over those gathered in the temple. Faces in the crowd revealed shock and doubt.

Kalif bellowed like a bull deprived of his cow and hurled the vizier's flail at

Ryker. He lunged forward, knocking Azad to the ground with a sweep of his arm.

Shield interposed himself between Kalif and Safia and Kalif paused and stared into his face. 'You . . . Shield! It can't be — ' For a moment he stood motionless, stupefied.

Shield spoke confidently. 'It's over, Kalif. You've lost so you might as well — '

Rage lit Kalif's eyes. He cursed and brought a gun up from beneath his robe and aimed it at Shield.

The crowd broke and surged forward, surrounding him, angry at his treatment of the Prophet. Hands clutched at him. Voices howled.

Kalif towered above the mob, a giant of immense strength. He clubbed men down, dragged others with him as he pushed forward.

'I'll kill you, Shield, kill — '

The drone of an aircraft engine in the night blotted out his threat.

Still hampered by the crowd, he lifted his gun-arm and aimed. Shield ducked.

In the courtyard beyond, Melody moved out from behind a stone pillar.

Torchlight showed confusion in the temple hall. She raised her rifle and waited for a break in the mass of weaving bodies and bobbing heads. She got a clear sight of Kalif's dark face and remembered the perfume seller in the bazaar; and there was no mercy in her. She squeezed the trigger and Kalif swayed and toppled at Shield's feet.

As she lowered the rifle, Al Hakim and his squad raced from the desert into the temple.

* * *

Shield sat at the desk in his office at 13A St. James's Square and thought: it's good to be home again. He looked at the glass swan-shaped vial on his blotter, the vial he had collected from Kalif's yacht after Al Hakim had taken charge. And he thought about his trip into the desert when he'd buried a small bottle taken from Kalif's pocket. Maurice Cole's perfume wasn't going to worry anyone again.

Melody had turned Suki loose and the

python coiled about her body as she danced a few steps on the carpet.

'I felt good at the *Blue Sphinx*,' she said. 'Maybe I'll take a cabaret job now and then, just to keep my hand in.'

Ryker leaned against the wall beside the window watching the plane trees in the Square; comparing the light with that of Cairo and composing a picture in his head.

They waited for Grevil to arrive.

It was the day after their return to London and, even after a night's rest, they still felt disorientated.

Ryker turned from the window with a brooding expression. 'Hakim's a lucky man. Not only do we nail Kalif for him, but he gets a girl like Safia to look after. And I reckon she'd be the grateful sort.'

'The Prophet came out of it well, too,' Melody said. 'He's a tough old boy who knows how to turn a situation to his own advantage.'

Shield lit a king-size and busied himself setting up a chess problem; he hadn't even told Barney or Melody about Ben Cowan. When he'd brought Cowan out of the underground chamber, he'd kept him isolated till he got him safely out of Egypt. Not even Al Hakim could have looked the other way if an Israeli agent had him brought to his attention . . .

Grevil arrived, a dumpy man in a loud check suit. His eyes glistened as they saw the vial on Shield's desk.

Shield handed him an envelope. 'The balance of our fees, plus expenses. They run high, but then we had a little trouble recovering your property.'

Grevil opened the envelope and blanched. 'High,' he yelped. 'This is robbery!'

Melody unwound Suki from her shoulders and pointed the python's head at him. 'Of course, if you don't want it — '

Grevil muttered under his breath and took a cheque-book and pen from his pocket. He wrote a cheque and placed it on the desk, snatched up the vial. He left in a hurry.

As the door closed behind him, Melody said: 'I still think I'd like to feed him to Suki.'

'This will hurt even more, I imagine.' Shield handed her Grevil's cheque. 'Ask the bank for immediate clearance, will you?'

'Could be there's not that much of a hurry.' Ryker looked thoughtful. 'He can't just take out the stopper and sniff — he's got to find himself a guinea pig first.'

'Well,' Shield said, 'coloured water never hurt anyone.'

'I'd like to be there when he tries it on,' Melody said dreamily. 'I hope she scratches his eyes out!'

THE END

We do hope that you have enjoyed reading this large print book.

Did you know that all of our titles are available for purchase?

We publish a wide range of high quality large print books including:
Romances, Mysteries, Classics
General Fiction
Non Fiction and Westerns

Special interest titles available in large print are:
The Little Oxford Dictionary
Music Book, Song Book
Hymn Book, Service Book

Also available from us courtesy of Oxford University Press:
Young Readers' Dictionary
(large print edition)
Young Readers' Thesaurus
(large print edition)

For further information or a free brochure, please contact us at:
Ulverscroft Large Print Books Ltd.,
The Green, Bradgate Road, Anstey,
Leicester, LE7 7FU, England.
Tel: (00 44) **0116 236 4325**
Fax: (00 44) **0116 234 0205**

THE WOLVES

Lawrence Williams

A war in which men die in great numbers in mud-filled trenches is regarded with loathing. Yet often the same people justify the actions of small bands of men who fight behind enemy lines. These men are rarely depicted as vicious and brutal. Instead, they are considered daring, surmounting incredible odds and hardships: should one of them be fatally wounded, unselfishly he will stay behind to hold up the pursuing enemy . . . In fact, the reality is somewhat different.

NIGHTMARE FOR DR. MORELLE

Ernest Dudley

Helping Interpol unmask the big wheel behind an international narcotics racket, Dr. Morelle himself becomes involved in a train smash, with unforeseen results. Meanwhile, Miss Frayle, his querulous and inimitable secretary, makes a flying dash across the Continent to help him — but is also caught up in the sinister tangle.

THE GLOWING MAN

John Russell Fearn

Under the cover of darkness and a violent storm, electrical engineer Sidney Cassell thought he'd committed the perfect murder. But immediately after pushing his rival to his death from atop a pylon, he himself is struck by a live high-voltage cable. Cassell survives the accident, only to discover that the electrical shock has affected his body strangely . . . Soon he becomes sucked into a vortex of murders and treachery, hunted by the police and unscrupulous scientists seeking the secret of his weird affliction.

THE WHISTLING SANDS

Ernest Dudley

Along with a large cash legacy, Miss Alice Ames had inherited the Whistling Sands, an old house overlooking the Conway Estuary. And it was here she began married life with Wally Somers — alias Wally Sloane, wanted by the Sydney police. To Wally, Alice and the Whistling Sands were just a means to the money he stood to gain. But when both had come to mean more to him than that, he became enmeshed in a web of deceit — and murder . . .